It's Raining, Storming Yet, Still Looking For Sunshine!

Angela Cross

It's Raining, Storming Yet, Still Looking For Sunshine!

Written by Angela Cross

Copyright ©2013 – ALC Productions

ISBN-13:978-0615860343

ISBN-10:0615860346

Cover Design by Allyson M. Deese

Interior & Website Design by Allyson Edits! Services

www.allysonmdeese.com/allyson-edits.html

No part of this book may be reproduced, stored in a retrieval system, or transmitted by any means without the written permission of the author.

This book is a work of fiction. Names, characters, places and incidents are either products of the author's imagination or used fictitiously. Any resemblance to actual events or locales or persons, living or dead, is entirely coincidental.

ACKNOWLEDGEMENTS

I would like to give thanks to God for my true existence, my parents, Barbara and Arthur Cross for representing true love and being my foundation.... I thank my sons, Dylan and Nyles Muzzall for supporting their mother in my attempts of parenting them as a single mother, my two older sisters, Teresa Mathis and Valayia Cross for leading the way and allowing me to learn from their mistakes and successes....

Much gratitude to all of my friends for their stories, support and encouragement. A special thanks to my friend, Lisa Porter for inspiring me to write this book and not accepting no as an answer.

DEDICATION

I would like to dedicate my book to all of the people, male and female that have gone through trials in their effort to find true love. Also, my friends and family that supported me through this journey.

It's Raining, Storming Yet, Still Looking For Sunshine!

PROLOGUE

What can I say? I never anticipated my life turning out like this. Two children; divorced and forced back into the dating scene at the end of my thirties. Me, Nicole Pittman the girl that all the guys wanted. Well, back in the day that is. Never would I have predicted myself to have married a loser. My life could have been perfect if that darn college sweetheart would have choked up his pride and married the gem I presumed myself to be. Of course, the whole college scene is where I woke up from my stupor.

There were so many girls that were pretty. I felt like just another number. A lot had changed from high school to college. I managed to join a prominent sorority which maintained me in the pool of the known. It's funny though, I never indulged in the college scene. I dated older and missed out on the frivolous years of partying. When I think back to those times, I feel as if even then, my will to be content in a relationship was too soon. I never explored multiple options while dating. The devastation of losing the closeness felt with the one man that I'd connected with through my college years left me in limbo. My ex-husband's charm won me over quickly with fears of dating again. I truly believe me the "relationship girl" wouldn't have known where to begin. All young ladies seem to have had a time frame of college, marriage and kids that roamed in my social circle. The excitement of my first proposal took off like the next major goal accomplished. Every little girl looks forward to the day she marries. My naive and very limited experience led me to believe all would be fine and if not, I would fix it. My "Miss Goody Two Shoes" persona was put through trial and error until one day it became more than I could bear. I had to get out. The end of my marital status found me traveling down roads I never imagined. A whirlwind of meets and dates with limited prospects of quality. How horrid this game is called dating. The funny thing is there are a multitude of avenues to do it and the results seem pretty much the same. This equally yoked thing is simply an image we've created in our heads of that perfect mate that may or may not exist. Do I give up hope or continue to expect great things? In the meantime, it's best to research myself and the foundation of which I base my ideals. Refresh… my term I use for starting anew and instilling hope for brighter days. My sunshine is coming and all rain and storms that come before me shall end. I reflect on all the negatives and wrong fits that have brought me to this place of relationship bliss. My new find is one of a kind and the connection that we develop is one hell of a ride!

Chapter One
Bad Choices

Today, I'm deep in thought, thinking of what my life would be like had I stayed married to my ex-husband, Brandon. I can't believe we made it through ten years of marriage. He wasn't actually my type, you see. He was tall, brown, and handsome as can be, with no direction. I was more accustomed to a man that was a little more similar to me.

He worked in the cafeteria at Trinity Hospital. I noticed him smoking and thought to myself, *yuk*. Listening to my friend, rant and rave about how she noticed him checking me out and how fine he was swayed my thoughts of cigarette disgust. I looked him over a couple of times, but wasn't sold just yet. The moment he finally approached me I'd lost every excuse my mind could possibly think of. Unfortunately, my girlfriend, Gina, whom we'd been visiting, had another week of recovery before she'd be released and that meant the chance of bumping into the cool, Smokey Joe of the hospital a few more times. I reluctantly said, yes to his request for a date night with me. Who'd have thought that would be one of the biggest mistakes a sistah could make.

Brandon was very charming and willing to please me at all cost. Even if that meant spending his paycheck trying to do so, literally. Early on I learned that he would be ill the moment his money ran out in order to avoid hooking up with me that day. However, being as naive as I was, I actually thought it was kinda of cute. *Awe, he's really trying to impress me,* I thought. I was newly employed as a social worker for a prominent agency and didn't feel love should be based on money. Truly, straight out of college and not ready for the real world. I'd been in love with a man who lived in my college town which was all of two hours away from my home town.

Larry was the love of my life at that time. I was devastated when our relationship ended due to the distance between us. Larry was my idea of a real man in any shape or form. He knew how to treat me and also, how to take care of his business. Only problem was like me, Larry was the youngest of his siblings and felt obligated to remain at home with his elderly father after other siblings had left and went about their lives. I believe the true issue was that Larry feared the distance in our age much more than the distance of our residency. He often referred to me branching out and finding myself as an adult and seeing what's out there before settling so young. What he didn't know was being with him was all I truly desired.

Sure, thirteen years was a big difference in age, but the brother was so me! Early on I knew that intelligence was an attraction for me right off the back. That's why for the life of me I don't know how I ended up marrying Brandon. Larry was adamant about teaching me some things like, budgeting my money. He told me to allow myself monetary clearance of at least three monthly bills. It stuck in my head to save and assure that there were at least three months bills in my account. He treated me like a lady. Larry took me out a couple of times throughout the week and provided me with gas money for visiting him all of thirty miles away from my college town. He bought me sexy items before I was even thinking of exposing the sexy in me. He was my first of meaningful relationships.

Brandon came at a vulnerable time for me. All the signs of don't do it were hitting me in the face. Lie after lie and excuse after excuse was merely dismissed as life carried on with me playing the fix it girl for my husband's ongoing disappointments. Still lusting after my college sweetheart yet, still yearning for some in town companionship. My love for my college sweetheart began to diminish as time away from one another progressed and the overly charming Brandon continued to represent in his absence. We did a lot of romantic things together. Brandon actually wanted to take me on a picnic. Yes. A black man with romantic flair. We frequented parks, museums, movies and diners downtown. Everyone agreed we looked so good together. Of course, that was truly important for a newly employed professional woman like me.

Who cared about the financial status of this handsome, charming man, Brandon was eye candy and that was all that mattered. Chocolate, six feet, wavy black hair with thick brows and beautiful eyes, slender built with a smile that said, "take care of me for the rest of my life." We truly had some good times together in spite of his work ethics. He was pleasant to be with, but undependable, and trifling, with whorish tendencies that I soon found out about. I overlooked the many children that he'd conceived prior to us and thought for sure he would be different when it came to us having children of our own someday. Things lasted for years with us having many financial woes.

Brandon had every excuse in the book for losing employment. Someone spoke to him like a kid, I don't feel well so I'ma just chill at home today and other exaggerated complaints or excuses on way too many days, and my favorite, I'm injured and can't return. He was infamous for the lies he'd told, but it just dawned on me that this thing with jobs was ongoing. The brother simply didn't wanna work. Ten years of ongoing madness. Some would say brother man whipped something on me, but truthfully our intimate behavior didn't have a whole lot of pizzazz.

We were two peas in a pod. Two words, traditional and matronly. Neither of us explored things out of our comfort zone. Oral! Are we talking dental hygiene? I felt like the sistah from *Waiting to Exhale* that seemed to appear relieved when the intimacy was done. Wasn't big on the whole sex thing. Well, two kids down the road and too many years later, I discovered I was tired and wanted much more than the tired, Smokey Joe that frequented the basement sofa. Things begin to change. I no longer found contentment in just having a man in my home. I wished for intimacy more than before, consumed myself in eating healthier, began to exercise and stopped turning down outings that led me away from my home. My husband didn't like company and never wished to go to anyone's affairs. As the years progressed things became more and more obsolete than I'd expected. We engaged less and less in activities with one another. We use to go out periodically. Watching sitcoms and blockbuster highlights was just fine. He seemed to really like children when dating, but more and more I saw his irresponsible actions with those he had prior to ours. A few years down the road, he showed very little interest in our very own children. Not to think that he should display a difference in the ones we procreated, but I was a damn good wife to him. At least show some favor to the woman's offspring that took over spoiling your behind where your mother left off. I guess that was our major issue. Respect.

I had no respect for my husband. He didn't possess the manly qualities that I needed to release my control over things. He had to ask me before buying a soda. I mean seriously. Another kid with the appearance of a full grown, capable adult. I suppose my berating and respect issues showed more than I knew. The man went from weekly, monthly to who knows when in offering a little TLC! I yearned for attention and it was no longer from him. I reflected on my feelings of resolve.

I believe there comes a time when we must grow up and be responsible individuals. Sometimes we hide from our greatest fears by pretending that everything in our lives is great. Over the years, I've realized that life is too short for pretending it's simply peachy. Faults need to be acknowledged and put in perspective.

We all want so desperately to be considered perfect or without flaws, but the truth of the matter is we all have issues. We wear masks at work, home and around our friends. Does anyone know who we really are or do they just think they know? Do we actually know who we are and what we want out of our lives? Years of experience in this life game and maybe, I still don't know what it is I truly desire. I do know that I do not wish to waste any more years being unhappy and consumed by the benefit of others. One thing that I have learned is that no matter how hard you try to be hard in any given situation, eventually you'll become soft. Many say what they would do if certain situations were to arise. Only when and if controversy shall come knocking at your door will they be able to suggest any action to take.

We are made vindictive by those who hurt us. Originally, you don't wish to be spiteful, but once suckered and then, still suckered some more, you have no choice but to grab what dignity you have left and hold on with dear life. I choose not to be hostile for he doesn't understand or care to understand my feelings of anguish. I believe a mother once said, "When you become tired that is when and only when you'll seek justice."

For when a woman is done that is when it is over. We often prosecute ourselves for the sake of our children. Children deserve and need good parents. With that said, it should be understood that one's mind should be at peace, free of worrisome issues, healthy and stable, ready to engage. If thy parents are unhappy so shall be their offspring. If we set unstable examples that is what we ask for them to follow.

It all started at the job. All of my female associates would buzz everyday about their love life and all that took place. I'd never heard so many graphic details, let alone experienced them. I tried to keep my composure, but the good girl in me was suddenly intrigued. I listened intently and couldn't wait to hear the next sistah share her tidbits about the male population and what works for her. Clearly there were men out here that were enticing their love interest with fun and true entertainment. Oral interaction never sounded so good and the thought of the sensuous touch of a man simply over powered me. I felt so lost and innocent all in one. I mean here I am a grown ass woman with no real experience. I've got babies to prove it. Prove What? I'd engaged in intercourse. Wow. My husband wasn't even interested in me anymore and for some reason I'd accepted it and believed it to be my size and not the blatant disrespect in other matters. Yeah, I was a chunky monkey, but I'd seen gorillas with more excitement than me. So, as a result of these new sexual urges I began to have, I began to watch my weight and shed the pounds. Wow, a whopping thirty pounds. I am doing my thing at this point, but still the Smokey Joe isn't amused or the slight bit interested. Come on, *really*. Still very little to no sex. I'm done. Melt down for sure.

Now, I'm going with the flow and simply doing our daily routine until ooohh. Dang, Mr. Buff and pleasing to the eye steps to my office. He is a case worker that works for the agency across the hall. As Johnny Gill says, *My, my, my.* Before I knew it he and I were talking and befriending each other like nothing was wrong. He gave me pointers on how to turn on my husband and what men saw as sexy and more. I found myself dressing for his approval and talk about transformation.

Here goes, I went from that matronly sistah that saw nothing outside of the homestead to self-conformed jazz puss accepting compliments from all. I was out of the flats and on with the heels, thrown from my pull-on pants to form fitting slacks and short skirts, plunging blouses with pushup bras and last granny panties were gone and boy shorts now, worn. Well, Brandon obviously wasn't taking heed to his newly transformed wife because he was too busy entertaining his own newly formed relationship with the young Latina, Kelly.

Kelly was not the most attractive, but catered to my husband's every whim. She worked in the hospital. A nurse that obviously knew exactly how to nab my husband's attention with her nurturing ability. He was definitely impressed. All I heard was his girl, Kelly this and Kelly that. One of my girlfriends tried to give me the heads up on Brandon's affair, but I saw all of the signs before anyone else. It's funny how people think they can roam a certain area where the likeliness of black people is rare. Brandon, dumber than a box of rocks decides to parade Ms. Kelly around a mall that I've gone to a million times. Who spots him other than my mom's nosey friend? He wasn't just there keeping her company as she shopped, but holding hands and displaying other affections, clear as day in the damn center of the mall. Really? This woman has come to my home and smiled in my face. Their scam was new job options for Brandon. Supposedly, Kelly had some connections that could help him land a higher paying position in the hospital. Well, he knew I wouldn't interfere with him trying to better himself. He expressed that he and Kelly were just cool and her boyfriend was ok with them being buddies. He even had the so called boyfriend come by with Kelly, of course to watch a basketball game. My eyes are not half shut, I clearly saw right through their thing. Brandon's jokes and every word seemed to intrigue the giddy fool. The other guy kept eye balling me as if he was hoping I wasn't blaming him. I said nothing. The clincher for me is how the guilty woman kept telling me how Brandon talks to her about how proud he was of me and how much he loved me. Now, don't get me wrong, he may have expressed something positive ,but if anything, he'd express how I have rode his back time and time again for not keeping a job.

Otherwise, their ploy of her helping him move up in the hospital would never have worked in her favor as an acceptance plea. There was some relief in my heart because I felt like maybe it was me that had felt the urge to stray. Sex isn't everything and maybe my husband had just become complacent with our marriage. He seemed so unmoved by sexual desires. I mean, yes, I probably contributed to his lack of interest with constant nagging, but now it is finally resolved for me. He had become smitten with someone else.

You know my mother always said, *"If you don't make him feel special someone else will."* She was absolutely right. I gave him havoc for not stepping up to the plate and she told him how great he was. I think that every marriage is a learning experience and for me it was marrying someone that was not on the same page as me. Brandon and I grew to love each other in a familial way and unfortunately, I had never thought I was missing out on anything until I saw the connection of solid marriages displayed before me where it is give or take shared between both in a marriage. The look on that man and woman face when they greet one another says, honey I'm glad to have you. I believe we developed a comfort of him being the slacker and me being the one driving. I had so much hope in my husband and for us, but things changed and we changed. The intimate value of the relationship had long been abolished from our marriage. Truthfully, I didn't care about the affair he was having because he had long ago stopped being intimately involved with me and our union was simply for the kids. I was strutting around and being acknowledged by my buddy, Brian who worked across the hall. Funny thing was Brian was married and unhappy, too. We were both married, young and shared the comfort of marriage, but saw our mates and ourselves change and become no longer a fit.

We laughed about how much time we spent at work and in the evenings entertaining each other. Whether it was via text, email or phone, we'd made a tempting connection. I liked him and respected him so much more than my husband. He was a self-made man, definitely not a bum.

He spent time engaging his kids and was financially able to hold down his household. My husband possessed neither of those traits. Oh and the brother had a great personality, which was a plus, and a trait that didn't Brandon possess either. I began to withdraw from my wifely duties and only find time to engage with my sons. I looked forward to evenings of engaging in increasingly personal and intimate conversation with Brian. Who knows or cares what kind of engaging my husband partook in late evenings he spent in our basement. All I know was he wasn't engaging at all with me. I believe he had other women making him feel good about himself and that Kelly girl just seemed to get closer and closer. One of my family members mentioned seeing him at a restaurant with a Latina and it didn't bother me one bit.

He'd also, been spotted with this midget girl that worked with him at one of his previous jobs. He called her his bud as well. I slept on that one because she was a midget and figured it was simply an odd friendship. I overheard him joking with his buddy about the thick bodies on midget women. At the time, I was oblivious to the expensive gifts and money for rides home this little woman had provided to him. Hell, I probably encouraged that affair right out. We no longer resembled a loving couple. It felt as if I did everything alone so, what was the purpose of a spouse? At this moment realization kicked in that we were simply complacent in our stance and the substance we once shared had diminished. I voiced my thoughts to him and found myself moving toward divorce full throttle ahead. I felt like the woman in the movie, Runaway Bride. What do I like…fried eggs or boiled? Here is where I began the transition of the new me in today's new world.

So many years I'd done whatever Brandon wanted and forgot about my wants and needs. I felt lost and didn't know where to turn. In the mist of all that was going on with me, my father was suffering from a terminally ill disease. My husband was barely talking to me, let alone a comfort to me at this time. I found myself latching on to Luke, a family friend that was overly available to me as a venting tool. I spoke to him about my father, my failing marriage, financial woes and my children. He was so there for me. This brother became my confidante.

We confided in each other personal marital issues and later, he'd expressed a crush he'd been harboring for me. I expressed how turned on I was by a guy at work that was entertaining my thoughts while Brandon had seemed so far removed from our marriage. As I confessed my desires for another man, other than my husband, Luke's interest began to develop more and more my way. I liked Luke a lot, but truly wasn't trying to fall in his direction. It just seemed like our closeness developed more and more as he continued to be by my side.

My mind moved further and further away from the interesting and inspiring Brian after he decided to transfer to a closer commuting location for the sake of carrying out his fatherly duties with his kids. Picking them up from school was quite a hike from where our office building was located and his running late frequently would cause them to be kicked out of their after school activities. Luke was more than happy to oblige my conversation and continue complimenting and flirting where Brian left off. Brian and I continued to be cool for a minute, but the absence of our daily flirting and conversations caused our communication to dwindle. Luke wasn't the pretty boy type, but definitely had swag as the young girls might say. His average height and non-keen features didn't take away from his cool upstanding attitude. He walked with an aura of true confidence. He knew exactly what he was doing. He made me desire him. I was hesitant at first for fear of my family getting wind of things, but had voids of a woman not being fulfilled.

Sure, Brian had started this along with those chatty women at the job discussing their every intimate detail, but Luke was going to finish it. My void was fulfilled by Luke. We texted and talked all the time. The first time was horrible. I had dreamed up this fantasy of love making taking place and everything from the thoughts in my head of infidelity to how big the brother's penis was sent me in a tizzy. I simply couldn't endure. He was too big. We kept trying although there was plenty of discomfort. Given the passion we shared and the experimentation of numerous positions, I finally took him like a soldier. I found myself so drawn to him. I wanted more and more to be with him, not sexually per say, but just him. We ate, shopped, and embraced with passionate kisses. He kissed me all over my body with delight. I felt sensations overwhelm my body with his touch. Sex, however, was months in between, but no matter what, we upheld our communication and friendship. We'd engaged all of four times over a year's time and our relationship became a dying phase. We both had other lives and could not keep this thing going. He played on an adult baseball team, attended all his kid's events and isolated me from his world on weekend's altogether. I became lonely as I was before and only focused on work and my boys. He knew that though Brandon and I had not finalized our divorce that I'd be open to meeting other men because he couldn't give me his time.

I felt like it was time to move on because I would soon be single and was not going to continue to frolic around with someone else's husband in addition to that, letting my family get wind of what I'd done. I sat silently thinking of the day Luke caught me off guard coming by while the boys were visiting their dad. I'd been standing in the mirror of my bathroom getting ready to go to a birthday party in my honor when the doorbell rang and it was him cool, calm, sexy and driven. I spoke to him as if I truly had little time and needed to head out as soon as possible, but I don't think he heard me because he stood right in back of me and began to nuzzle on my neck. My neck is so darn sensitive. I think I'd momentarily lost it because the next thing I knew he'd caused me to lose my bottoms and the man's touch was all over my body. He had me mesmerized. All I remember is the bathroom never looked the same after that day. Whew. That brother was smooth. It is funny how you think back to people you could have dealt with at more opportune times, but passed right by for whatever reason. Luke and I were both single and available souls at one time that knew one another in a totally different light. I believe it was the flash of a Cancer Man. I didn't pay much attention to zodiac signs at that time and simply use them as silly references, but wow.

I recall him being a bit self-absorbed and a bit too much for me. My demure character would have been eaten alive back then. His frequent visits to our home as a family friend back in time will now be replaced with memorable moments shared only between him and me.

***

Overdue Intimate Weather

You grow withered with disbelief that any single freak can restore that weak feeling that you have when you must release, the fore longed hold you kept to stay strong, the content feeling that long grows old, you wait for the thrill for which seems to be up hill, but the everyday life has kept you astray from the you, you so truly desire to be…is it the strength of being a mother that lines your endurance or prolongs your unselfish being…could it be shame shown if the true you were embellished or foreseen by any naked eye…maybe your spousal rules do not allow you to peruse the more worldly you.

Whatever it may be shall you seek to be free, free to express the sensitivity a woman desires, the sensuous breeze of his breath on your neck, the passionate familiarity of that first school kiss, and that unforgettable mesh of two bodies entwined…a simple brush of the flesh untangles the hairs on your back, that nervous yet, non-calming look releases chills up your spine…what's grown old becomes rekindled, seeking only that girlish memoir of the very first time…don't become consumed by that consistent sought out weather rather create your storm and keep it warm for your intimate weather is long overdue.

Chapter Two

Newly Single and Open for the kill

It's summer and hot. Luke and I still talk almost daily, but the flame had long ended months ago. I had to release the anguish, pain and guilt I felt associated to our closeness and move forward in my life.

I'm dressed to impress with a gold and cream colored print skirt and a brownish top that accented my cute brown sandal perfectly, slightly made up face, big beautiful legs and nicely polished toes and a smile to die for. I'm on the way home from work and decide to do a quick return to the department store when I find myself standing in line being admired by the funniest character I thought I'd ever meet.

I'm thinking, I've gotta get home to my boys. Brandon and I were just waiting for the final word. Matter of fact, Brandon had moved on to new prey. He told me all about her. He was truly impressed. She was a fireman paramedic and head over hills for Brandon. Little did I know this chic would become his new wife in a matter of months! Wow... Court was set for two weeks and we'd both be free. Brandon contemplated getting back together and brewed up enough courage to ask me if I'd want to try again. Thing was he was about to jump in yet, a third marriage with someone else, but was making certain that this meal ticket was dead set on moving on first. I quickly responded, "I believe we are making the right decision."

All these thoughts are compounding me as I impatiently wait in line with this silly brother making all kinds of faces at me like he just saw a beauty queen or something.

"Hey Sexy, I'm Rick."

"Nice to meet you, I'm Nicole."

"Is it possible to get your number so that I can get to know you?"

"Sure, why not."

Rick was chocolate, six foot three, and very charming. Swag was an understatement. Street, definitely. Something I definitely wasn't use to. What the hell, he's funny. This whole date and befriending thing is new to me. I'll test the waters and just see what happens.

Oh My God, during the first conversation with Rick he exposed everything. This has to be a joke. This brother put all of his dirty laundry out before me and I liked the honesty. Talk about game. Well, I'd dealt with a liar for ten years. He had been incarcerated for bank robbery scams. He'd been on drugs and currently lived with a woman which things had gone bad with because she realized her preference was to be with another woman, but after much communication they had managed to savage their friendship enough to live out the term of their lease. I must have been truly vulnerable because I allowed myself to fall for him totally. I overlooked his extremely ghetto tendencies, took him in my world with children and all and let him totally monopolize my world. I was turned on by his dominance and persistence. Hell, I'd been the man for as long as I could remember.

He was that cool guy that never had interest in the uptight sistah like me. He rocked my world better than any man I'd been with. I knew he was not acceptable in my world, but I desired him more than I had any man before. Why couldn't I keep this street fool that made me feel so good? For one, I couldn't trust him. Rick had women after him, blowing his phone up, giving him whatever he wanted. He'd scammed my foolish behind and after many threats and insults he repaid me because he didn't want to lose me. The brother whined about needing money for a boot on his car that never existed. He was a damn good, "con". I'd totally gotten myself caught up in this "street type brotha."

He wasn't good enough to be around my kids yet, but he was fun and entertaining with them as well. There were several things that occurred that said let him go, but my heart and feeling sprung wouldn't allow me to. He knew that all he had to do at that time was bed me down and I'd surrender. Just the thought of him saying, "Baby, why don't you go and clean it up for me?" did something for me. I get chills just thinking of what that saying meant. I couldn't think straight until the roller coaster of passion ended.

I think of how dominant his character was and how I let him empower every inch of my body. I shuddered at the thought of what escapade he'd take me on next. His love making was not only passionate and unselfish, but a true know all of everything that made me pant and squirm. I tried so hard to ignore the bad in this relationship because I knew that passion for me would never be the same. After several months of hearing, hoping, waiting on the "B.S" to end, I threw in the towel. He began stalking me. Rick came to my job with flowers, blocked me in my garage forcing me to talk to him and called me consistently for four months after the relationship had ended. I'd gotten a police report after he'd threatened me and still had to get an order of protection against the fool. A lesson learned, play in your own lot. This was a lesson that I will always remember, unfortunately. Later, I found out his game tactics he'd played on me. His so called roommate at the time that he'd told me was gay was his woman for two years and she expressed putting up with my demands and calls to their place because he'd convinced her that my youngest child was his and that I was simply crazy. Way too many lies. I began to think of our relationship and what it entailed. I felt embarrassed and ashamed for being played. I asked myself, "Why must we endure things that are momentary?"

Is there truth in everyone needing a learning experience? Originally, I had major doubts in dating this man. He revealed things to me that I'd never accept. After assessing the connection felt when engaging in conversation or simply being around one another, I sensed that God placed him in my sheltered life for a purpose. Never could I accept the many flaws I encountered within my spouse but yet, I embraced a man who was worse off in a sense than the spouse of whom I disregarded. I've come to learn that we are in search of something that fulfills our voids. For me, it was never about the finances alone. The man that steps to me must have some backbone and be able to read and understand what I'm about. I've never been superficial, materialistic or driven by what one could do for me. Instead, I have always been a feeling person; sensitive, emotional, and comforting, intuitive to Nicole's personal needs. Financial, well, that's another story. I've always been self-sufficient in meeting my financial needs. However, this self-sufficient attitude seems to be a deterrent from meeting the appropriate companion with similar financial status as I.

In dating and being previously married to a man who as the "Good Book", refers to as not being equally yoked, I find myself becoming resentful, yet accepting of the wishing, wanting and waiting syndrome I like to call it. First, there is the wishing. All along you're dating a loser or let's just refer to him as the less fortunate and you are wishing that he could be what you want for him to be. You imagine him with a good paying job, proper etiquette, and great with your children and all into you. While all along reality is staring you in the face telling and showing you that he is what he is. Quit dreaming and move on. Ha. Now, your lonely hormones kick in and you are vulnerable. He's clearly not Mr. Right, but definitely, Mr. Right Now.

He knows he has nothing to offer, but what he does have is charm. He will make you think you want him. Whatever you like, he does too. You are the best thing that has ever happened to him. He can't believe you are actually interested in him. He flatters you and can't seem to get enough of you. All the things that you wished a guy would say, he says. He totes you around as if you're the number one prize. Boy, don't you want him even more? You figure, what the hell. I'll see him for a little while. What harm could that be? We're just having fun. Oh no, you slipped and fell.

Now, that just for a little while fling has you all loved up and sprung. Girlfriend, you are stuck, you think to yourself. I was very aware of the situation's reality, but wishing and waiting for more and more to expose itself. He promises things will change and he gives you a bag full of "I'm gonnas." He follows through as much as he can in hopes of leaving the old sponsor for something bigger and better. You now feel the desire to wait. Oh no, the waiting ordeal is for sure the kill. He's gotcha. You are in it for the duration and may or may not ever get out.

You stand whole heartedly next to your man and all of his excuses and employment woes. Will he ever be on top of his game? You grow weary waiting, you use every family, friend and prominent person you know to network for him. For some reason or another, nothing becomes permanent or ever works out.

You then begin to think he doesn't take his jobs seriously because he has me, his number one sponsor.

Why should he have to perform and step up to the plate when his woman is so capable of holding down things without him? Now you once again, see him for what he is, the loser or much nicer term, the less fortunate. You now find yourself stuck with this irresponsible fool who adores you for one thing, the resemblance of his mother. You resent having to take care of him.

You waited for your time of spoiling and financial support along with other responsibilities only to find that you've been got. He may really love and care about you, but wouldn't you if the roles were reversed? It's so hard to say that this is true in every situation because the scenarios could very well work to your benefit in the long run or take advantage of his opportunities and become of equally yoked status ,but no longer have a desire or need for me.

The moral of the story is it's always best to match apples with apples. No one should have to hold down the fort alone. Never, never, again. How could I have been so foolish for him? It took so much for me to release my heart from the man I desired thus far, more than any man I'd before. All I can say is the man lived the reputation of a scorpion male *passion beyond passion* and I would do my best to stay clear of his kind.

At this point, I'm hurting and taking no one's feelings into account, but my own. My next encounter is once again that of the taken. Yes, he is married and of course at this point, I'm divorced all of a year's time. Nonchalant and ready for fun is my new motto.

While awaiting the arrival of my girlfriend, I find this gentleman by the name CK all too funny. Long story short, my girlfriend is having hair issues and decides not to come. That's right literally faking a sistah out. In the meantime, CK is definitely sparking my interest. He is my favorite kind of chocolate. Dark. Nothing better than a chocolate man in a crisp white shirt, jeans and nice kicks. He is ordinary, not that ooh wee fine, but a cool all his own that makes the intrigue present at first meet. It must be this whole honesty thing again. I tell you after being married to a liar for ten years. I'm a true sucker for the honest male. The brother is just as laid back and smooth as a piece of crème pie. We chuckled and hit it off with conversation right away. He tells me he isn't trying to divorce his wife, but he likes what he sees and enjoys my company. I nod with agreement. He tells me he can offer me a great time and his friendship while I continue my journey for Mr. Right. I look at him strangely and respond, "I don't think that's a good idea."

He says, "Ok, let's just be friends and tonight think about my proposal."

As he leaves the club, he turns around and asks if I was hungry. I looked at him twisted and he responds with badge in his hand, "Girl, I'm a cop." Still leery I look at his friends who are edging me on, one of which knows my cousin that works the field. I asked what he was hungry for and he gave me a devilish look. He then, responds what about some shrimp? I bashfully respond shrimp would be perfect. He tells me to get in his vehicle and I respond, "Do you think that is appropriate, Mr. Married?" He looks at me with a grin and tells me should you be worried if I'm not? We drove all the way to the other side of town for shrimp and continued our evening with a quaint little bar where we shared more drinks. I had the time of my life with CK. Months went on with us hanging out and enjoying one another's company.

I've repressed feelings. Feeling lonely and trying so hard to break the loser husband type, then, totally loser screwed up rebound, Rick. Yet, here I am again with yet, another bad decision. Falling for the, oh so nice, whorish cop who's more attentive than many of my male encounters except of course, Rick. I like him. I enjoy the way he treats me. I never been one to believe that a man needed to pay for my time, but I do believe he should date you.

I allowed CK to do whatever he wanted for me because his married behind shouldn't have been frolicking around town with me anyway. I shouldn't have been lured by his chivalry either, but he's so cool. He acts as if he's my man. He treats me out for meals, kept my weave hair bill paid, donated to my bills if I came up short and even surprised me on Mother's Day with flowers. He and I became confidants and friends. I have to fight any emotions that I may feel because I know I can't have him. After things he has shared, I truly don't think I'd want him anyway. He is a cheater.

Our friendship or fling dwindles as he finds less time to be with me over the summer during his many family vacations. I now, feel neglected and *I'm not liking it.* Good Bye married men. I'm done.

Now, it's back to analyzing my situation and figuring out my next move. I guess the problem I'm having is that for so long I've been upholding the "Good Girl" image and now, I've had a little taste of bad in terms of my transitioning from marriage to this single stuff. Everyone knows that "Nicole" has *always* had a man. Hold up not just a man, but the one that everyone else wanted. Hmmm, how in the hell did I fall for Brandon? Oh, that's right he was all of nothing spectacular, but handsome. It's funny how tables turn. It's hard out here after being in hibernation for ten years. I know that I can't do another Luke or CK. I'm way too good to play second for anyone. Even the con, Rick made me feel like I was his number one chic. I'm confused and now, I'm losing my position on relationships with my girls. They are starting to wonder if I really can pull anymore. Wow. Don't they realize it's harder out here now that we are older, I've given out subtle hints to my coworkers that finding a man to date is becoming more of a chore than one of the simple pleasures of being single. One coworker said she'd suggest on-line dating because she knows of several couples that met on-line. The others agreed and started sharing personal stories and those of others. Well, for the most part the stories were entertaining and sound good enough to think about for my next venture. Of course, there were those sistahs that would scare ya for sure. Girl, it's some crazy folks on-line, you better meet a man the old fashion way. And what exactly would that be. Humph. I guess that would be food for thought. I'm truly trying to find the fun in this dating game, but I really wish I had my stable life with the love of my life. Of course that would have meant marrying my college beau instead of Brandon.

Although, when I think of my college sweetheart I think he was right, I needed a lot more of life's ugly experiences in order to grow into a mature woman. As I think of the place in which I fell after a failed marriage, I wonder how the flaws preceding divorce could have been prevented. My emotions were on fire and someone was needed to help put that fire out.

Change in pace was my first disgrace with men that weren't appropriate for the likes of me.

***

Desire to Embrace

I wish to be touched in a way I've never been touched before…I wish to explore life in ways unthinkable…I wish to become one with the true me…I wish to be sexy and unpredictable to thee…I wish to be fulfilled mentally and physically…I wish to indulge in life's intimate pleasures, more experienced…I wish to explore the wild side of me…I wish for gentle embraces with strong man hands that guides me graciously…I wish to be all I aspire and beyond what others expect and wish for me.

Chapter Three

Realization and Loneliness

I have never had a hard time meeting guys as a teenager and young adult. This dating thing can't be that hard. I read somewhere that a break is needed after each relationship and that it's smart to date yourself in order to find out what it is that you truly like. I suppose dating me and stealing time away from my boys for me won't hurt. Food. Everyone loves food. I will entertain myself with a breakfast date at Q's, a famous breakfast spot among black folks.

If I can make it through a meal without being judged or feeling weird I have accomplished a major breakthrough. As I walk in the restaurant, I have a gut feeling to turn my butt right back around and exit before someone spot me and realize I'm not as on my game as people may assume. I spot a couple of old women together. They look at me with pity, as if their thoughts render poor man-less child. It's as if I have been caught with a scarlet letter engraved on my chest. There's couple's engaging and enjoying their meal over quaint conversations and a few older men sitting near the corner. The waitress politely sits me near the corner as if I'd preferred to not be seen. I thought to myself, "Nobody Puts Baby in the Corner." As I sit, I look around and it appears that there are more couples and families than I'd pictured. I turn to a greeting nearby and it is the old men in the corner.

"Hi Sweetie, would you like to join us?"

I shyly reply, "No thank you" with a genuine smile.

They retort with comments of a pretty young thing sitting all alone and eventually I hear their conversation return back to their next fishing outing. I order my usual the French toast, egg beater with cheddar and crispy fried bacon with a small juice. It feels so good to be waited on. I mean without the distraction of the boys bickering and stopping every moment to cut pancakes or blow food for the children.

It's so serene. Well, that wasn't too bad. I did it, ha! Who needs a man or companion? Of course, this won't happen too often because my oldest is only eleven years of age and the youngest is seven years of age and the chances of Brandon's trifling behind picking them up is slim to none. He believes that he is punishing me.

The boys return home and I am consuming myself with everything from their karate class on Saturday, to football practice every evening. Washing clothes, cooking, homework and laying down the law is a part of my everyday life. Can't remember the last time I've been on a nice date.

Time seems to be truly passing by so fast. Football Season is over and more of my time is being freed up. Brandon has still not asked for our sons. That bastard. He is now remarried and wouldn't you know the woman he married has no children. Well we all know what that means…he's her only child and there's no room for the offspring he produced. Eight months has passed and still the loser hasn't picked them up. He began calling to check on them two months ago. *Really. The choices we make truly hunt us.* I'm literally screaming for some alone time. My friend volunteers to take my children to a gaming spot with her boys and finally I have a day to myself. I contemplate on washing dishes and making a big meal to last a couple of days when the thought crosses my mind to have date number two with myself. Hmm… 12iI decide to go to the show to see an old movie that I figure no man, would've wanted to see anyway. Surprise, Surprise, there's more couples in the show than I'd anticipated.

I do feel awkward, even a little weird. What the hell, there's plenty of other popular movies much more suitable for couples. Oh well, I'm here now. I sit watching the movie and munching as quietly as possible, but all of them were still glaring at me. At the moment the movie ends, I sashay my pretty ass right on out of the theater and smile to myself as their men look me over, and I think to myself your turn will come girl. Although it was hard for me sitting amongst the couples in the show it was still invigorating because I managed to challenge myself again. This alone thing definitely takes time. I enjoy shopping alone, but dining and entertainment is different. I want a companion that wants to do cool things with me like: plays, trips, exquisite dining experiences and just hanging out from time to time whether it is his place or mine.

My children and I do breakfast after church every Sunday. I'm sitting and reminiscing about the time I went alone. I love my boys and it is just as entertaining having them with me. It's an emptiness that is stuck within that makes me long for a man. I think of the hot, steamy, passionate moments I shared with Rick. The brother had some dynamite in his stuff. The way he used to kiss me, my clothes magically fell off. The mere thought of him riding me and licking me lavishly on my neck, circling my breast, gliding his tongue along my side and kissing my navel so succulent. Oh no, he couldn't possibly stop there he had to divulge my inner most spot, my open wound of pleasure. He kissed my most feminine area lightly and then before I knew it he'd went there and back taking me all in with such delight. The boy was dangerous.

Mmm… I get excited just thinking of that passion. It's time for mom to have some adult time.

Chapter Four

New Age Dating, Here I Come

It seems like as the months go by, I've tried everything from dating myself to over indulging in activities with my sons. I'm becoming irritated. You see, the thing is I have become a woman with needs, now. I wasn't feeling the whole sex thing during marriage, but I am on fire now at thirty-eight years of age. I can't go giving my stuff out all willy-nilly. I need a consistent partner that is feeling him some Nicole. I have to at least, believe that he is looking at future possibilities with me. So, the being in the relationship thing is pertinent for me to be able to satisfy my needs. The on-line thing isn't looking so bad at this point.

My very first online dating site, Expressions of Color is a black dating service that a friend has recommended. I'm looking over photos to find the perfect one. Not too sexy and not to plain Joe. Ah ha, the perfect picture is one I took when posing for friends before we ventured out for a night on the town. Not sexy, but cute. I download and my passage begins. Oh my God. Fine. Who'd have thought that there were so many fine men online? Dang. What is wrong with them? The first couple of weeks are amazing. It's so entertaining. I have looked at many profiles and have received so many winks, smiles and hellos. Every day there is someone new checking you out. My head is swelling from all the attention. By week three, I've met a few at local coffee shops ,but quickly forgot them the moment I returned home to my computer to find even more kind words said and more attentive conversations arising. I met with a guy at Burger King for a Coke and he is seemingly shy or bashful as we sat and chatted. I'm thinking how in the hell can he be bashful around me with a body like that. The brother's body was like *bam*. This guy seems real aside from the chats and flirting that I've had in the past. I'm more than curious. He and I began to talk all the time. He is constantly asking to hook up with me. My computer is becoming a neglected toy. He is dominating my time. He and his son engage with my sons and it all seems so right. He goes by the name Disco because spinning music has been his side gig for many years.

Disco seemed to be so into me. Everything that I ever wanted. His personality was a little over the top, but wasn't anything I felt I couldn't deal with. Over time, I realized that Disco had some issues stemming from his past experiences. I became more than a lover and friend, but his personal social worker and a loan officer as well. You see, when I invest my time in someone I put my all into making things work and he definitely took my all. The brother was on me like a squirrel on a nut. He called me twenty-four/seven and kept up with my every move. If I went to the rest room I found myself still on the phone with Disco. He wanted me at every party he'd done. I felt like Disco's groupie. Now, we all know that a sistah wouldn't have put up with all this madness if he wasn't putting it down. Disco had a crazy temperament, but never when dealing with me. I affectionately called him "The Hulk" because of his rage. Little things would cause him to blow up. The man was already of intimidating stature of six foot five inches tall, wearing a size fifteen shoe. He wasn't my favorite flavor of dark chocolate, but the brother's body was bad. He said he'd done some body building in college for a couple of tournaments. He was very different from what I expected of the man of the hour to be. He was sweet and kind to me at all times, but our personality differences caused a lot of friction.

When I first started dating him, we decided to become invested in one another after a month's time and removed our profiles off line to avoid distractions from others. He expressed some money concerns and wasn't quite in a position to date me. I jumped in knee deep with Disco's financial issues way to soon. He had a nice quaint home and a couple of vehicles. He had a SUV for everyday use and a pickup for his DJ equipment. I didn't understand why he had to possess two vehicles. No wonder he couldn't afford to take me out. Mortgage, car notes, child support and more consumed his flow. The moment I found out about the rip off loan store he'd gotten himself involved in I thought I'd die. Talk about check a brother's credit history and financial obligations first. Whoa. My heart went out to him and being the only lady in his life I felt compelled to help him get on track. Of course, then, maybe we could actually date without him feeling the need to find coupons for every place we ventured to. I took a plunge and allowed Disco to use my credit card to pay off his $1,100 worth of debt. He was so diligent about paying me for the next few pay checks until the debt was resolved. Excellent. Well, almost. Here's where the problem started. Disco and I would frequent the mall or stores in general together and I'd pick up items for my home and boys and think nothing of it. I started to notice Disco feeling comfortable with throwing things in my cart as well for him and his son. At first, I didn't say much because as said before he always paid it back, but I started feeling like he'd always assume that I had him financially. I wanted for him to say, I really need this, but I'll get it when I get paid. Not, can you front me on more than a number of occasions. I mean really, did he think I was a bank? I expressed to Disco how I felt and he respected it for a while and expressed his gratitude for my looking out for him. When his television broke he asked if I could loan him the money until he got paid and that was when all hell broke loose and it wasn't a sexual encounter, begging or pleading or anything that the brother could say to me before I closed that chapter without a turn of the head. You see, he had begun to resemble Brandon to me. Of course, he wasn't trifling like Brandon. Disco was honestly, very responsible in terms of paying his bills, but had gotten himself way over his head. I just felt like he truly needed to find security in the work place before it was too late to land a job other than spinning records that would provide him with benefits. Disco was a hustler and I needed a man more stable in the workforce than that. That's when I realized I wanted someone more financially sound like myself. I really wanted things to work between us, but Disco wasn't a big kid person either and it was only a matter of time when he'd be released anyway for mean mugging my baby. The two of them were not a match at all. He got along fine with my oldest, but that was probably because they both displayed similar characteristics of rage. I think it's time to say good bye to once again phenomenal sex. Dag. I can't seem to keep my sizzling love life content. Truthfully, I think that I wouldn't have stayed in my last two relationships this long, but the intimacy had me climbing walls in both of these relationships. I didn't consider what CK and I had a relationship for the record because our thing was brief and he didn't belong to me. He just gave me some much needed fun until things began to get complex. Both, Rick and Disco just so happen to be SCORPIO MEN. Next time I meet a Scorpio male, I will be running for my life. The passion is more than I can bare and indeed hurting to part from. Something about me connects to the Scorpio Man. As I reflect on my experiences with the last two men my poetic flow tells all I know...

***

Scorpio Man

The Scorpio man comes with man complexities, their strong willed, choosey and daring to be near. They swoon you with affection and interest that's sincere. Their forceful and direct with little need to be made clear, never cross their path wrongfully for they'd come after you with a vengeance and that shrewd business demeanor threatens all and any that disrupts their path...when it comes to this be prepared to feel their wrath. Though we fear their aggressive display, their sensitivity is nothing to determine dismay…they love hard and will keep their interest on their toes with constant persistence that simply overflows, you should never feel neglected because their attentiveness shows… the glow on my face is because I've got a Scorpio Man in place… Yes, I must hold on for the ride and simply walk in stride for I know turbulence is on their side…when it comes to passion they're the best, there is no other that has passed the test…they please you with persistence and know what you need ,but their desire for intimacy must be appeased…if sensitivity isn't met their at an all-time fret…make certain to be upfront because when it comes to them expressing their going to be pretty blunt… choosing to engage with such can be a bit much ,but the outcome of passion is so sensitive to the touch… so embrace the Scorpio Man and treat him gently as can be, if he's feeling you… that you will truly see.

Chapter Five

A Journey through a Series of Sites

After dating Disco, I felt drawn back to the original, fresh, new start of dating where I'd met him. I recall the number of good looking men on that Expressions of Color site. I went to visit with my friend and speak openly to her about my wanting to do more online dating and she looks at me sheepishly and says, "Really?" while contemplating her next statement. Tisha was very judgmental, but I respected her candid advice.

"Why in the hell would you wish to go back on the site that Disco was on?"

There was the possibility that Disco had returned after our breakup. I thought.

"Why won't you experience different sites monthly to assure that you've covered your bases?"

"Tisha, I like that idea." I'm thinking this could be a test of some sort to see if the online dating is truly all it is cracked up to be. Tisha rattled on and on about the horrors and those that actually found success online. All I could think about was me.

I'm downloading my profile to Shades of Brown Connections. This really is taking off to a good start. I'm being tagged and asked out for meets very quickly on this site. It's kind of generic compared to Expressions of Color, a little cheaper too. I first meet Tyquan, a man of intelligence that lives and shows he has purpose in life. Now this is a deep brother and a little younger than myself I must add. He's a gentleman, employed, in school and a great conversationalist. I like him, but not feeling the true sparks that a sistah is looking for. I will keep him on standby because he may prevail to be less aloof once he's done with school. In the meantime, I do a quick meet the following week with Darren, a real estate broker who had me meet him at a bowling match. The brother is not fine, but has a style all of his own. Kinda pimpish if you know what I mean. Something about our conversation told me he was kind of controlling and jealous. He verbally attacks me at the bowling alley for being polite. "You are trying to holla at my boy and you are supposed to be here to meet me?"

"No," I explained, "just responding hello back to him." He mean mugged me for the next ten minutes that I remained before I decided to make a quick run for my car. I never responded to the calls there after and he soon got the message that this chic wasn't interested in the crazy pimp type. It seems as if I'm on a roll with crazies because I now am juggling between a boatman from Canada whom seems quite strange that I won't even contemplate meeting him and a crazy purple heart veteran who must be disabled because he's refusing to meet me after great conversation. I soon dismiss that crazy as well. My strangest yet, is the former marine who takes me out a few times and shows a slight temper each time. I'm catching on to patterns that signal abuse. We go to the restaurant and I politely allow him to sit facing the door. He says, "If I tell you to walk ten steps behind me will you do that, too?"

Hmph, I guess that is some sick humor that he felt was warranted. As we leave and head back to the car, I walk in the inside to allow him to walk closer to the street and he stops and immediately addresses how stupid it is for me to go through all these means of dignifying a man's stance. "First of all if someone begins shooting I'm going to save myself first and then, when all is clear I'll check to see if you are ok and follow up with the hospital if need be. So, truthfully there is no reason for my walking on a particular side of the street."

I'm thinking, how touchy. Our first date was much better even though I'd asked him not to bring his dog to my home and he did anyway. I refused to go on our walk with his pet. Besides he was a vicious dog. I won that battle. However, returning home from the third date he speaks of how this thing between he and I just won't work because I'm too superficial.

"What?" *Who the hell does this jug head think he is?* I politely retort, "excuse me, I don't understand. Why would you call me superficial?" His response didn't even make sense. He explained that everything was about something being cute or me trying to look cute. Uh duh... I'm a female! One of the many favorite expressions is how cute something, somebody or whatever is. Of course, I too, want to look good for myself and the appreciation of the lucky man I'm with. *I mean, really!* Now, a sistah must be going crazy because for the last few weeks I've been entertaining conversation with a Jamaican Man from Cali. His pictures are so appealing to me. Tall, chocolate, conservative and did I say handsome as hell. Whew. Boy would I like for him to come to my hometown in the big city and rock my world. The weird thing was he and I carried on as if we had a relationship, although we were miles away. I'm here in Chicago and him, California. I began to get envious and so did he of others in our lives, being of opposite sexes. There was no way this thing could work, but we were definitely attentive to each other's lonely needs for all of three months' time. I truly wanted to meet him, but the thought and reality that this man would truly be coming to bed me down with no trace of past or current dealings other than the words expressed through my finger tips and daily conversation was scary to me. We soon had a heart to heart and realized that this thing or void we filled was best to end because we both were getting too involved in something that was doomed by distance from the very start.

More meetings and craziness are still to come. Tisha is coming over to discuss more options for my life. I think she is becoming intrigued by the crazies out here in Chi. Seriously, this dating cycle can be quite entertaining for those not enduring it. My girlfriend, Gina believes that I should just be patient and wait for a good man to come into my life. Humph. Easy for her to say when she has her good man. Tisha sashays into my home as if she owns the world, not realizing that it's only me she'll be sitting before. Funny, that is exactly why I stay on my game. Friends like Tisha won't let you begin to slack. "Girl, what the hell do you have on? No wonder you haven't found Mr. Right yet."

I giggle, "For your information I've been cleaning all day. Now, what's your big plan?"

"Two more sites for you to examine. I have heard nothing, but good things about both. They are a little pricier, but you get what you pay for." I frown with doubt. I suppose I could take her suggestions, after all what have I really been doing ,but fishing in a pool of players, liars, strange ones and still there's nothing show stopping or worth my time.

Tisha is more than certain that the more options I have the more likely I am to meet the right person for me. A friend of hers spoke very highly of the two sites, Serendipity Online Service and Perfect Partner Online Service. I believe everyone knows about them both because they are advertised on every commercial break of any major television program and both sites filter to diverse groups of people. The commercials are quite annoying to be honest. Selling the perfect fairytale. It's like dag; I would like to enjoy my program without being constantly reminded about my sucky love life. Tisha and I continue to chat about the most ridiculous meet and greets that I've encountered. She is literally cracking up as I tell the stories behind each one. "Girl, this guy Casey is built like a pear and obsessed with his ex-wife. He speaks of her in every conversation and I find myself finding out more about her than him. We met out a couple of times, but he really is a downer. I decided to pass. The social worker does not wish to do service on days off."

"Nicole, he must've been a good looking, pear shape brother otherwise you wouldn't have wasted your time."

"Yes, he had a very handsome face, chic." We both break into giggles. I began to tell her of this fat, cocky fireman and how his attitude stunk from start of date to finish and she recalled the name. "Girl, my guy friend, Eric works with him. He says he only likes white girls. I guess you are pretty fair, but I guess not fair enough for his dumb behind." I look shocked, but dismiss it with a simple sigh and carry on with my stories of meet and greets, the last two, Ron the whorish cycler and Frank the vegetarian. "This Ron character has the audacity to tell me that my stuff isn't special and that no one's going to date me a number of times and not know whether it was good or not. Girl, I must've snapped, I told him he could take his raggedy ass right back to these women that gave it up to his trifling behind before because the shop here is closed and so was this meeting."

"Girl, what did he say to that?"

"Awe, girl I was just kidding with you. Just wanted to see where your head was at. I like you, you different."

"Wow, Nicole that is too funny. Men are awful."

"I know right. The other guy, Frank that I was telling you about was so polite and eager to meet from our phone conversation. When I see him I'm immediately intimidated by his size, like, uh giant. We began conversing about our jobs and I fill him in on the role of a social worker. He tells me stories of being a plain clothes cop and all seems to be going well until we began discussing the menu."

"Why would the menu be of concern?" Tisha asked with a look of confusion on her face.

I began, "I like my bacon crispy and their sausage is excellent here." Girl, he looked as if I was among the minorities, not in race, but my selection of food. I politely asked, "Is everything okay?"

"I guess we never discussed food. I'm a vegetarian."

"Oh okay, is my being a carnivore a major problem for you?"

"Uh, yes."

"Really."

He began to explain the negatives he's researched and how important it is for the woman he becomes involved in to be on the same page and suggests we finish our meals and just become friends. Needless to say I won't be seeing or talking to him again.

"I'm thinking how curt."

"Whoa, you mean to tell me dating has gotten that complex to our choices for meals? That's crazy. Who'd want to be with someone as anal as that anyway? So glad I'm not out here with you in this mess. You are too good of a person to have to go through such scrutiny from these assholes."

"I know Tisha, it is hard."

"Well, try the two sites my girl recommended and let me know how that goes for you."

"Yep, sure will."

I sit drinking a glass of wine, finishing the bottle Tisha and I had started and remember when dating was so easy for me. Boy, I surely thought I was the stuff for sure back then. Now, in my late thirties approaching forty, it's no joke out here for those of us single, be it never married, widowed or divorced. I reflect on all of the many girlfriends I have and their thoughts about me being single again. One of my girlfriends retorts, "Well, while you were married we were going through dating hell and now it's simply in reverse for you. You've always had a man and now, you see what the rest of us had to endure."

Another girlfriend says to me, "maybe you are just too picky. You know you are a lot older than the last time you were single." Many friends have tried to tell me to just be patient and it will come. On the flip, I'm one of those girls with male friends as well. Their take on things are a lot different from ours. One male friend says, "Girl, you better work that magic and put it on that man." Another looks at me sheepishly and says don't give up your goods to soon. While others retort, women need to learn to just chill and give up on those labels, and brothers won't feel so intimidated. My hang out male buddy wants me to be accessible for hanging so he is always negative in regards to other men. My play brother, Aaron says he believes I want too much out of the men I meet. He says men don't date like they use too. We just buy you all a little something, something or give you a little cash and that seems to suffice. Most women are ok with that, but you bougie types expect so much more and that is why you keep finding yourself alone.

"Change with the times, girl."

I will say everyone has their perspective, even the comedian guy, Steve that wrote the book on how to snag a man. Maybe I'm simply a hopeless romantic, but I still believe there are good men out there. The thought suddenly crosses my mind of my father saying, "There's no such thing as a good man." I took it as if he was being comical because my sisters and I all looked at him as if he was the main exemplar for which we base a good man on. The way my dad treated my mom is exactly what we three girls of his wish for.

Serendipity Online Services. Well, this is different. I have to go through so much crap before I can even browse the selections. Oh yeah, the price for this so called excellent site is double that of the others. The site practically dissects me as an individual first. If I didn't know what or who I was, I'd definitely know after this experience. If someone is interested in you, they forward questions to you and depending on your answers and the answers to questions you've posed it would be determined if interest continues. All of these interventions before you can actually email and talk freely. Most of the men on here hold great jobs and high end positions, but their profile pics don't leave a lot to be desired. No, not the fine brothers like sites before. More square and less attractive. My first meet is with a guy I refer to as Jimmy the cricket. He is unbelievably thin. I'm scared I may swallow him with the rest of my entrée. He is very nervous and has no children. Open for anything. Appears somewhat anal and not very personal at all. I'm bored to tears and at first sight I knew he wasn't a future interest. I find myself rushing through my meal and talking about my kids to spur immediate disinterest. I feel bad, but with my thick and voluptuous body, we both know there is nothing this tiny lil fella could do with me. He should have been on the petite only site. Wasting my time with his little self. I began talking to a new male prospect off the site and after viewing his pics, quickly realize he was a "Can't do". He just so happened to have a photo with family and he is the brother of a former classmate of mine. They won't be hating on me if things don't work out. Besides I wouldn't want all my friends to know I was dating online. Me, Nicole who dated one of the cutest guys in high school, I think not. I already have to deal with my college sorority sisters all within long term relationships with the majority being married. The most elite and first acknowledged sorority for black women and I'm a "Can't Get It Right, Sistah Amongst Men", we won't be displaying and putting my relationship status and style of dating out there. I mean, there is a twist to this and that could very well be that maybe I truly am a little picky. I now, meet Reese and boy am I nervous. He's very attractive from the photo and has it going on financially. He is a corporate manager for a very well-known company and we seem to hit it off during the few conversations we engaged in. Our first meeting finally arrives after much juggling with his busy schedule. He has chosen a neighborhood Italian restaurant not far from me. As we greet each other he appears larger and older than his pictures suggest, but I'm still willing to see how things end. As we began to discuss our interests and lifestyles he sticks to the subject of his daughter and the importance of her liking the women that he dates. I try to focus on his subject of choice, but realize that the excessive saliva in his mouth is starting to distract and annoy me. He expresses that she doesn't have a good track record in terms of women she found suitable for him. I listen intently as I realize where this date is heading and as we resume the date I've made up my mind that he's not for me. The gross saliva issue put the icing on the cake. Who could imagine kissing him? After our date he calls a few times, but soon finds out that I don't have the energy to entertain foam filled mouth or his child. Done with this site.

Perfect Match Online Services, here goes. This site reminds me a lot of the last one I encountered. A lot of unnecessary information to access me and seek the perfect male. Blah, blah, blah. The men aren't as ugly, yet most seem to be gainfully employed and the fee for this site is maybe a whopping five dollars cheaper. My girlfriend, Cory has dated outside of her race and has encouraged me to be open to others this time around so I've taken her advice. I met a variety of men on this site, but those I seek interest in with a brief, hello are not as eager to return the greeting as fast or at all. I feel there are a lot of picky people like myself on this site and I'm thus far not impressed with my results. The first meet I get from this site is a

Latino male. He is brief in conversation as we chat over coffee. He makes no excuses for his preference. He wants a chocolate sistah and that I am not. Wow. I decide to try one more interracial experience with a white male. This is tough because I truly like chocolate men. There are a few exceptions like, John Travolta in the movie, Basic and the guy they call "McSteamy" from that popular doctor show every one watches, but other than that there is a slim chance for attraction. White men are much more attractive with the rugged facial hair look that they despise. However, I received several hellos and can we talk from this Caucasian male so I am opening up my options. After much pondering with myself I go out with the white male prospect. Our first date is to the same little quaint Italian restaurant, but he decides we will do a show immediately afterwards at a local art center near my home. All goes well until I hear this man's story. He has a cat. I dislike cats, profusely. He tells me how he has a child and how her mother abandoned them because of his and her use of drugs. He overly expressed how clean he was and for how long. I notice him fidgeting throughout dinner. I'm so ready to go. Oh no, still to come the show. We enter the show and the first person I see is a neighbor. I want to scream he's not mine, but he tightly clasped my hand with his clammy fingers and I'm feeling like crawling under a chair and hiding. His hand does not feel good. Yuk, clammy is not fitting for me. I work with a large white and Latin population and they wouldn't believe the story behind this date. Yes, a white male displaying all of the negative stereotypes quickly placed upon the black male. Drugs and employment hardships. I hear so many ignorant black women expressing finding themselves a white man as if to say white means they are better. Don't people know that you cannot get caught up into stereotypes because we all have some bad seeds within our races and they don't dominate one culture alone. We've got ghetto blacks, white trash and gang infested Latinos. No culture is clear of bums or less desirable ones. I've since then, hooked up with a few other males that unfortunately weren't a fit for me and now it is time to go back to where I found myself semi successful with the relationship with Disco. I know Tisha warned me, but just maybe

I will find someone quickly and be able to take a break from the madness and frustration. I will admit it can be kind of entertaining when getting started. I'm back on Expressions of Color and already I've got 10 hits. Now, that's what I'm talking about. More eager brothers and cheaper to meet them. I see a brother that seems interesting, but another darn cop, ugh. His profile indicates he's looking for a pen pal. We begin talking through messaging and it's pretty cool because we aren't rushing the meet thing, but conjuring up interest for sure. His name is John Johnson. I like him thus far.

Mr. Johnson is the man of the hour. John is a little taller than the average height, standing five foot eleven inches. He appears to be clean cut, pretty decent looking not quite chocolate and definitely not bright like me. His demeanor is laid back and possibly a little uptight. Our first meet takes place in his office because he works within the detective unit so he isn't on the street like the regular beat cops. His hours vary and a lot of overtime is required from him. He's been married once and accrued children that are now grown from his marriage. He lived with a woman for some years and they had a son together. This child is his main and only priority outside from his job. He has expressed to me how much he likes me and that he will make the time in his busy schedule to get to know me. He asked that I be patient with him because women before have not been able to withstand his situation. He and his child have such a strong bond. His son Junior is his only boy and he plays year round sports that of course he must attend. Now, we've begun fitting in dates, but now I'm feeling like the overly understanding blonde chick that is always pushed to the side. His hours are mostly evenings and his weekends aren't the typical every other weekend visitation by the non-custodial parent. He gets his son every weekend. Major kudos, right? Well, again what about me? I decide being the proactive social worker that I am, that we need scheduled evenings. He seems excited about this idea. I find myself really trying to make this thing between John and I work. Tuesday, Thursday and Sunday are our scheduled evenings together. Although he is in my life it hasn't been that easy. John loves the way I pamper and cater to him, but the moment things change, compromise or even the slightest whimper of disapproval of something on his end is expressed, he explodes and may even require a cool down period of a day or two to digest things. His idea of bliss is to have things favor his way only. I figured if I continue to treat him like a king he would eventually see some of my desires and wants as being important enough to compromise for me. Wrong.

"Nicole, just give it time." He asked of me to be patient on many occasions, but things were starting to bother me about our relationship. I did everything I could to make our thing work. John was a workaholic because he was determined to be there for his older children in college who still needed financial support. I too, have my children first in mindset, but he took it to an extreme. I did have issues with his weekends with his son because he never allowed us to hook up together with our children. He felt he had to protect his son from pain in the case of things not working out. Of course I had issues with bringing men around my sons if I wasn't certain where things were going. My sons respect me and that's the way I hoped to keep it. Our scheduled time together was evenings after his work day. Considering he got off at ten pm, his arrival to my home was after my sons were put to bed. Our schedule was perfect. On days that John came to my home, I made certain he had a hot plate of food and a sexy vixen awaiting him. That would be me of course welcoming him at the door. I made certain I was smelling good, looking good and ready for him to devour. John's eyes lit up like a Christmas tree at the mere presence of me. I often tried to surprise him with little trinkets I knew that he'd like and made certain that he was pleased royally in bed. He loved the way that I made him feel and I loved catering to him. He took me out on occasion, but not as much as I'd liked for him too. Holidays, birthdays and other engagements were rare for him to attend either due to the job or his son. He gave me a pretty pricey piece of jewelry for my birthday which truly felt as if it was a symbol of his love. At first, he made appearances to the most important things like, Christmas dinner at my home and my birthday party, but other engagements weren't made for the most part. That really agitated me. I felt like I was a good woman to him and deserved more from him. I put up with his jealous and controlling ways. He wanted me front and center when he called or visited. As time went on I thought he'd want to get to know my children considering our time together was late nights on the down low without my son's knowledge. He never seemed to be quite interested enough in what went on with my boys and me. His only concerns were that of his children alone. I mean, he visited during day hours a few times, but not often. I needed more than just the three times a week of intimacy shared between us. I wanted a companion that would be more accessible to me. I spoke with John about coming over earlier on Sundays so that we could designate it as a date day for us. I didn't care if we'd just watch television together, but time spent outside of the bedroom to enhance our being around each other in more normal settings. I'd started feeling like hot sex was all there was confirming the love we were professing to one another. He whined about his schedule, "Nicole, why must you mess our good thing up? You know I work all day long through the week. I've tried to show you I love you with nice gifts and when I've had time I've taken you out. Plus, J would have a fit if I dropped him off too early on Sunday to his mom."

"I'm only asking that you take your son home a little earlier and spend some quality time with me. Maybe get to know my kids and think about doing some things with all of the children."

"Honey, give it some time. We've been together seven months and I don't believe J is ready for sharing me, yet."

I listened intently and after promises of trying to compromise failed, a few months later I found myself letting go of our relationship. Truth be told, I felt as hard as I tried to compromise and understand his warped sense of reality he should have tried harder to make things work instead of becoming angered by me wanting and expecting more. His stubborn behavior and bad attitude soon showed itself more profound than ever. John could be a little abrasive, like hanging up on me if he disliked what was being said or if I hadn't agreed with him, but the breakup caused him to truly show himself. He took the breakup hard as did I and began with personal attacks on my character and appearance. No he didn't have the audacity to call a sister, Porky. His ass is truly done. There goes any hopes of ever bedding down this sistah here and to think, I kept it sexy for him on the regular when we were together. Hmph, the nerve of him with that bird chest of his. I guess I'd never expressed my dislike of skinny men. Boy, am I glad that I found out what an asshole he really was. I mean yes, a sistah can definitely shed some pounds, holding down a size fourteen, but it has never been a problem with any man that I've had as a love interest. He even had the nerve to retort, "I even considered a future with you." So glad I didn't stick it out any longer with him. His head line should read, "Online Psycho can't take rejection or opposing viewpoints." So glad I woke up from my stupor with that fool. His bitterness caused me to stay away from the internet. Not sure if I'd visit online prospects again after the craziness. Just left a bad taste in my mouth. I'd never been insulted by a man in such a way as John had done. He talked about my physical make up and made me sound as if I was a cow. He used my insecurities against me and for that I'd never forgive him. I get admired on the regular for my voluptuous shape ,but even I know depending on the day, week or even the year it fluctuates and at times I am showing the desperate need of shedding pounds, but how hurtful it felt to be purposely reminded of something I struggle trying to maintain on the regular. What a jerk. Since our breakup, John has tried to apologize and take back the many negative comments that he assures me were said out of anger and his need to hurt me ,but deep down inside I know that I will never have anything else to do with him.

Truly, I believe he should consult someone about the way he behaves because I'm convinced now more than ever that he is unstable. Counseling would probably benefit him. How on earth did he make it this far in a police district puzzles me. I am reflecting now on the special parts of him I loved with realization that his temperament was never fitting to my mold. John was a Leo and believe me they are a piece of work to deal with. I felt so dearly at one point in my life and I saw him as a joy…

***

A Leo Man

It's intrigue, it's wonder, it's unrealistic to have such feelings of glee…Entrapment is an understatement for the emotions escaping me…I'm scared, yet, cautious, for could this be God blessed me with one who fits the mode so precisely… He's that unknown gentlemen that takes his time and walks in stride…no rush, no hurry, no mistakes in path…he appears of no nonsense and will roar if caught in his wrath…he's mature and not complacent to any lure… he's smart and meticulous and recognizes what's worth the endure…he possesses a heart that is genuine and pure…He's determined to do things right…with many temptations testing his might…he's hard working and stays employed ,but willing to make the time for something more…he acknowledges a woman in its form, beaten or withered and gone through the storm…He embraces her softness, her expressive way, that feminine and poise stance that she portray, her intelligence is no threat because too much surprise his wits are expressed and much obliged…He does not see blindly he confronts his appeal… he sees something special and knows it's for real…He's strong, self-assured and expressive all in one… he's competitive and on track proving never to be out done… a true servant, mentor, do right guy, they say…exerting his time and energy in his work every day…so focused and diligent , yet deserving of play…I see him treading slowly ,but coming my way…the excitement, the flutter, the unraveling joy… the vision of a real man, oh wow I mustn't toy… On point and up right I just met my match…convinced to somehow let body and soul be attached.

***

Boy had this image changed. The roar of the lion, I first saw as gentle became a vicious animal with no tact.

Chapter Six
Street Meets

If this is an indication of what being single means then, I better hurry up and meet my mate. I have decided to take the boys on a trip to Florida to visit my dearest auntie, Boney. We, black folks know we can come up with some nicknames for one another. My aunt had been asking for us to visit with her for a while, but being a single mother of two takes extreme budgeting skills when your ex-husband does not stay employed long enough to contribute. This is why we never made the trip until now. I have been single for over three years and the guys stepping my way have warning signs posted on their faces saying this one ain't going places, that one isn't fast in races and last he has committal fears don't go near. I needed a getaway and my Aunt was the perfect for bringing on a little cheer. In the months to follow my break up with John, I'd met some characters. Partying I've met a few. One of the darkest brothers I'd ever seen starts speaking to me as my friends and I along with other females in the club eye ball him intensely. The brother went by the name, Smokey. I'm minding my own business hanging out with my girls at a graduate chapter fraternity party, and here walks in a show stopper. Chocolate with a white, crisp collared shirt looking as if he'd stepped right out of Jet Magazine. Cool brother from the south. I liked him immediately, but of course he'd been dating someone and wasn't available. All I wanted to know was why the hell he had taken up all my time at the club that evening, when he knew he wasn't available. All the women envied me all for one evening of false pretenses.

The next day, I found myself thinking of that dark, chocolate brother all day. My past time has become spending money these days whether on a trip to Florida or simply shopping to keep busy. In three years' time, I have probably wasted enough money to pay a couple of month's bills. I know I'm seriously out of my mind. All the while, I'm beginning to humor myself with attendance to the fraternity's monthly events. I meet a couple of whorish brothers that clearly aren't on anything other than themselves and getting laid. This is truly for fun and seriously a joke for single women with hopes of meeting someone. I'm starting to get bored with it, but socializing with friends is keeping me entertained for the most part. Just wish I could keep my hand off my darn wallet. I'm browsing the shoes in the department store and stop to try on a pair of classy ass, Michael Kors when a tall, Mandingo walks up to me for conversation. Ooh Wee. He is a tall glass of chocolate milk. As I listen to him answer question after question, I find myself more uninterested than someone with the flu being enticed by food. He had five kids and a mediocre job. Now, what the heck was I going to do with him other than carry him as I'd done for years for my ex-husband, Brandon. There is no way in hell I will be that foolish again. A man must be able to take care of himself. All within the last two months, I've met "think-nots" on the regular. I'm picking up a couple of notebooks for the boys at the dollar store and a brother is sweating me for a phone number. I thought about what my friend said to me about being overly picky and reluctantly gave him my number. As I walk away he begs for a hug. I turn to give him a church pat and he grabs me. The smell. Not fresh... Ugh, didn't he know? I'm appalled at the thought of dating an unclean man. Really. Who does that? Asking for a hug, knowing he hadn't bathed. I live near the local drug store and everyone in the neighborhood and their mother is in and out of there. I've met a number of men that were either "think-nots or fake". A cute guy followed me around the store to tell me he thought I was attractive. After talking to him I find out that he is married. I meet a guy in the drug store parking lot on another occasion and hit it off with him big time. He never called. Wow, not only was it a waste of my time, but a realization that he needed confirmation that he still had it or could still score for whatever the reason. Separate occasion, but again the darn drug store and here comes, too old, but persistent. I figure I don't have any prospects why not. He asks to meet out for coffee and I swear I believe he'd switched places with one of my girlfriends. Gay, Gay, Gay. I should've known from the mannerisms of his swinging hand. I tell you meeting on the street can be just as shady, discouraging and crazy as meeting online. Whoa, the drug store must be my spot because this brother here is fine. I'm looking at his shoes, jeans, button up shirt with his leather jacket and clean cut style, I'm totally digging him. He smiled at me across aisles and he seemed to have had all his teeth. Oh well, leave it to my picky ass to spot an unsightly one on the side. I can't help it I love a man with pretty teeth. I figure it wasn't major because he can always get it fixed. We are literally standing for what seems to be an hour talking before we head off to our separate ways. The brother asked for the contact info. Yes! I'm in. *Oh darn, been through this before. He may not call.* Shut yo mouth, two hours later, an unknown number appears…oh yeah, it was him. Again, we are talking and truly hitting it off like, Ben and Jerry. Day two, he calls again and we both sound so excited. The conversation becomes more intense and he's expressing how he knows how to treat a lady and he likes to get all into what's his and whether it is oral or anal, he likes to fulfill her to the utmost. Screech... Did the brother just say anal??? My radar must a flipped a switch. Ok, now every woman has their limits or shall we say they're, Oh Hell No's". I had to dig further ,but as the brother tried to clarify and express that it wasn't a deal breaker, but if I was prepped properly and the mood was right I might enjoy it depending on my feelings for the person giving it. I'm thinking what part of "No." did he not understand? Normally sex is not expressed this soon, but he tried to slip that anal bullshit in on me real smooth. I carry myself like a lady and clearly don't appear to be some hoochie mama that will do it all. I mean don't get me wrong I love sexual activity, but my voluptuous backside is not substituting for my vagina on any given day. As attracted to him as I was and the engagement in conversation prior to, I no longer could view him as a date suspect any further after the Freudian slip of what the brother really had in mind for me. Maybe I'm too uptight but again, that is my ultimate sexual, "No." Besides all of my friends that have allowed some fool to do it, all agree that it hurt like hell. This sistah here is simply not into pain. Moving on to the next prospects to come. You Mister Nasty One have failed Nicole's Passion Do's and Don'ts List.

My mom's friend tells me the story of how she met her husband. It was quite entertaining. She found it very hard meeting someone special and decided to throw herself a birthday party that required all of her guest to bring one single male to the party. She'd had three prospects before the party had ended. The one that stole her heart was the one that stayed when all others gave in and headed for home. They seem like such a great match and have been married for years. After sharing the story with friends, many volunteered to hook me up. Rule number one, never ask single friends to hook you up and number two, make certain those hooking you up knows you quite well. One of my girlfriends works for the post office and she brags all the time about the number of men on her shift. She is by the way single herself. She tells me she has two men that she wants me to meet. The first man is definitely not my type, but Felicia pleads with me to give him a chance. She tells me, "Girl, he treated his last woman so nice and he would do the same for you. He's been seeing this girl that is not into him and he really deserves better. I'm going to give him your number." The guy gives me a call and truly seems nice, but wishes to come to my home to meet me. Felicia assures me it will be fine. The moment I see him, I feel like a giant marshmallow.

He has a small frame and not my type at all. Does Felicia know me? Dag. I listen with a nonchalant facial expression masking my face as if to say please excuse yourself from my home and move on to something or someone new. He spoke of the relationship he was engaging in and how he would like to open up to someone new. All I heard after a while was blah, blah, blah. I felt like a kid again watching Charlie Brown. No one ever knew what the hell the teacher was saying. Felicia felt so bad that she wanted one last chance to make it up to me. Everyone knew I'd played Cupid for every last one of my single friends at some time or another when I was involved. It was payback for Felicia and a few others. Felicia's next guy is totally opposite from the first. Fat and definitely too old. I was through with her selfish behind. I'd hooked her up with some decent brothers. None of which were fits for me. Well, the moral of this is your friends will never hook you up with something good because they would want them for themselves. I will never ask a sistah to hook me up again that hasn't found herself a mate first. Speaking of sisters, my older sister's boyfriend says his buddy knows a nice guy that may be a match for me. I scream with delight. My sis will not let her man hook me up with a monster because she knows me and has seen the men that I have dated. My sister, her boyfriend and his buddy come over to my house while we await this mystery man. I feel so excited. When I answer my door I thought maybe he had the wrong address because I know that my sister and her man didn't hook me up with grandpa. He truly put me in the mind of Sanford and Son's character, Grady. This man was definitely not ready for the diva in me. He barely opened his mouth. What in the hell? He warmed up slightly once around everyone else, but he could barely look me in the face. He seemed nice, but was all out of tune with dating and should probably have been hooked up with someone closer to his age. As I walked him to the door he said it I didn't, "give me a call if you ever want to hang out with an old man."

I smiled and said, "Sure" knowing damn well I wouldn't be calling grandpa for a date. As I returned to my sis, her man and his friend, I shot all three of them a dirty look and we all fell out laughing. My sister had never met him before, or she'd have been hurt for that one.

My boy Travon hooked me up with his friend, Corey. Travon described him to a T. He said that he resembled a famous football player and he truly did. I liked Corey, but found him to be a little cheap on our date and later found out that Travon had forewarned me that without the hat he no longer looked like the famous football player. The truth was that with his hat on he wasn't bad looking at all, but with the hat off it appeared to be a bad dream. Corey had a receding hairline that caused him to actually look horrible without the hat. As politely as possible, I inquired about the possibility of him going with the bald look. He not so politely responded, "I'm not cutting off my damn hair for anybody." I just looked in shock. I wondered what hair he was speaking of because the little figments of scattered naps on his head could hardly be referred to as hair. How do you say hair in singular? A strand here or there. He expressed that he could grow on me and that I should never judge a book by its cover, but when he repositioned himself in his seat I noticed a tattoo of a female's name on his arm. I then, knew that this was not a man in the same class as me. On several conversations with him he asked if he was going to hit it. Trying to keep an open mind, I politely asked, "hit what?"

"You know girl? When we going to stop playing these games and let me make love to you like a real man is supposed to."

"Oh, hell no. First of all, I don't know you and we haven't even gone out on a real date." I then, found myself giving him the let's just try being friends spill. He was a little more roughneck than I could do. I thanked my boy, Travon and listened to a few more comments of how good the brother was and gave my no thank you speech and regrets. The next encounter takes place at a friend's husband birthday party. I suppose my girl and her husband figure this is a guy's party and Nicole will definitely like one of the guys that is supposed to come. First of all, my friend should have told me about the brother other than he is nice and will probably treat you nice. At first glance, I already know I don't like him for me. Something appears feminine. He is skinny. Ugh. He is very articulate, which is a plus, but I'm simply not feeling these long braids down his back. He is a graduate from an astute college and yet, he has just returned from Africa and is a Vegan. Really? I don't think so. The brother didn't seem to be enthused by my looks either. He was probably thinking of my fair skin and wishing for an African Native with brown skin and all natural attributes. I'm sure one look at my chemically processed hair and by golly I'd blown it. Two good people don't instantly vibe; there must be something of common interest. That was very nice of them, but I think not. Now, my friend Joe was a Muslim brother and had every intention to hook me up with someone nice. I trusted his efforts. Joe saw something in me the first time we'd met. He delivers purified water to the building from which I work. We bumped into each other one day as I found myself tired, anxious and desperately in need of a wake me up cup of coffee. Our office has a kitchen set up down the hall where we keep all of our snacks, coffee and other needed necessities to keep the day moving smoothly. Normally, we simply give a brief greet and occasional small talk and keep it moving ,but today,

Joe is full of inquiry. I couldn't imagine why because the wedding band on his left hand was clearly not hidden. He wanted to know what a good woman like myself was doing single. I explained to him that men are just not like they use to be. I married a man who was no more than a handsome face with loser qualities. I thought he had potential, but later learned he never wanted to work and provide for our family. So, in a nutshell, I found myself cutting ties and starting anew with my two boys. I continued to go on and on about what I'd accomplished and what I possessed and before I knew it the Muslim Brother had stopped me dead in my tracks and put a halt to my boasting.

"Beloved," he'd refer to me, "you do have a lot to offer, but maybe that's part of the problem. You may be coming off intimidating to these brothers."

I snarled, "That's insane."

"Well, try taking it easy on us. You seem to have a little bitterness within."

"No, I'm just tired of meeting losers."

"How about I look into something for you and get back to you?"

"Whatever, Joe. Good Luck."

"I know a few good brothers." Joe quizzes me about my likes and dislikes and the following week he tells me to expect a call from a guy he knows from a school he delivers to. He assures me that he is a nice, church going brother that is interested in meeting a nice woman. The guy's name is Clyde. Ugh. Clyde? Really? Doesn't sound attractive at all. Joe says he fits my stats.

Clyde and I have our first conversation and so far he sounds alright. We both speak of what a great guy, Joe is and talk about our lives. After a couple of conversations, we plan a first date. Clyde asked to take me to the movies. Of course, I didn't think the movies would be the best first date because it wouldn't allow for face to face communications. Clyde is a heavy male with a generic representation of what today's hip apparel and overall appearance would resemble. In other words, no initial style or appeal. However, everything seemed to be going fine during the show. Clyde politely opens my car door as we began saying our goodbyes. He looks at me fondly and asks if he could get in my vehicle so we could talk a little before parting. I agree and think to myself had he proposed dinner, we could've been able to talk and gaze in one another's eyes to see if we had any chemistry or vibes. Clyde gets in says a few basic things and the rest is a blur. The man is like an attack animal. He is all over me in a matter of seconds. I'm appalled.

"What the hell are you doing?"

"What's your problem? Joe never said you were a virgin. We are two consenting adults."

"I'm sorry, but you've got the wrong sistah. I don't roll like that. I don't even know your ass and you are all over me like an octopus."

He seemed annoyed, "no hard feelings. I will give you a call later." Humph, I know that will be a call that I will avoid. I couldn't wait to let Joe know what a creep his church going friend was. "Beloved, I'm so sorry. Please allow me to make it up to you. I really thought he was a cool dude. I've got one more buddy that I'd like you to go out with and I assure you he will be a gentlemen. Joe's friend, Olsen was pretty cool and definitely a gentleman. We were brother and sister in our Greek organizations. We hit it off right away. Olsen took me out to dinner at a very popular Caribbean Spot. I loved it. Olsen was an entrepreneur. He owned his own business and knew how to treat a woman on a first date. Joe explained that he was a very busy man, but definitely single. After our first date, we spoke here and there, but nothing significant. It was almost like a parent or a friend checking on me when he called. I swallowed my pride and assumed he wasn't interested or had some unfinished business he was tending to. Nevertheless, Joe felt very empathetic to my manless ordeal and thereafter, persistently spoke of all my man issues being resolved with me just joining the Muslim faith. Here's where our union of my personal life took a halt. I love Joe like a brother, but there was no way he was going to talk me into changing my faith in order to find me a man. Really, who does that?

It's time for some exhaling with friends. I have invited my friends over to let loose and I'm picking up appetizers at Willy Wild Wings when a group of characters arrive and approach me at the bar. I'm patiently waiting on a variety of wings to feed my hungry guests when Mr. Funny Pants himself approaches me. Funny Pants walks over and takes a seat next to mine as he sizes me up before he verbalizes the appropriate line needed to approach me. "Hey, hey, this woman over here is trying to get close to me." I giggle and continue to nurse the drink placed in front of me. His baritone voice is quite entertaining. I look him over slyly without looking him directly in the face, catching a glimpse of his face as he turns to address his audience that's obviously getting a kick out of his toying with me. He's average height, about five foot, nine inches tall, with construction worker attire; a stout or rather husky build and has a face that reflects a distinct attractiveness all alone. He's kind of cute in a comical kind of way. He introduces himself as DeAngelo and says it in such a way that I know he is lying. I introduce myself as Nicole and offer him my card.

He takes a look at the card and laughs as he holds it up to his boys. "Yo, she thinks I could use social work services."

The guys laugh and refer to him by another name. "Aha, so your name is Greg?"

"Yeah, yeah that's it, lady. You got me." As I take my order from the bar, I look into his eyes and drop my purse accidently on the floor. Greg picks up my purse and hands it to me.

As he hands my purse to me, he whispers in my ear, "I'll call you later to make sure you made it home safely." I smile and walk away giving a wave to him and his boys.

I'm shocked. I'm well into entertainment mode with my friends, sharing wine and a variety platter of wings and my phone rings. I answer and it's him. Oh my God, did I doubt myself? I didn't think I would hear from him, again.

"Lady, I see you made it home safely." His voice is strong and deep. I can barely contain myself hearing him on the phone. My friends are wondering who's on the phone making this silly grin appear on my face.

"Yes, I am entertaining some of my friends."

"Awe, get back to your company and we can talk later. Give me a call when your company leaves."

"Ok, will do." Later, my friends leave and all I can think about is calling him back. I anxiously dial the number and quickly hear him answer. He sounds busy.

"Hey, Honey you think I could give you a call back?" I figured it was a little late. I'd probably get his call the next day. Wow, Greg decides to call me two days later and I just decided I didn't wanna talk to him. He will now be waiting for my call. I give it a day and call only to hear a voicemail. Another day goes by and I call again, but this time I leave a message telling him it was nice meeting him, but now that I see he's playing games, I'll pass. Unbelievable, men. I forgot the likes of him and deleted his phone number. Meeting men is just something I do. Be it while I was online, hooked up or on the street, there will always be some guy.

***

Feeling Me

I met him once, but wasn't sure if he was on much…so I took a pass and dismissed his whole stance…another day, months later I find myself taking another glance…caught by surprise unknowing he's the same, for his aura stands strong and enticing with music in his name…I'm shocked and mesmerized for it couldn't be the man I dismissed, so easily…he's confident, humorous and entertaining all in one… he's attentive to my needs and God's answer to my pleas…I shiver at the thought of him being all that I sought…I found him, I'm scared, could this really be, the man I stumbled upon is really feeling me…behold those of past that slept on this gem, your weak stepping to is way overdue…a gentlemen, a man of passion, a true delight has flown in on one rigorous flight…his charm, and manly display is undefeated in every way… I'm without words, my expressions are at a halt, my emotions are in an uproar, for I feel him in my every thought…he's delicate, yet firm and leaves me with no feelings of concern…there's an attraction like a magnet that has me wanting him more, my heart flutter's with excitement and giddiness galore…I trust him and want him and have no shame for he's my main player scoring in this game… I feel desired and adored with diligence ongoing…He's definitely feeling me and my glow is shining brightly for the whole world to see.

***

The poem, "Feeling Me" are my reflections of my second time around meeting, Greg.

A couple of months pass and I'm doing my routine, tending to my boys and occasionally entertaining or getting out with my friends. My girl, Noemi is in the mood to hang out one night and agrees to go to one of the sports bars I enjoy going too. It's been a minute since I've been out and momma can use some flattery tonight. I'm excited because this evening is one of which the bar will host with a popular band group that plays live jazz on select nights. Noemi and I enter the sports bar, it's a moderate crowd and we see the band is setting up. We sit off to the side and eyeball the crowd. Oh Yeah. Tall and handsome with chocolate color walks by and I'm thinking, nice. Noemi decides to bother the poor man and before I know it we are joking and chatting with him. In the mist of all the action, a guy sitting at the bar catches my eye. While tall, dark and handsome takes a walk to order some food, I hunch Noemi and tell her the guy at the bar looks interesting and familiar. "He's kind of cute and looks more my type than this guy."

Noemi looks him over and says, "Why won't you say hello to him?"

"Nah, he's just interesting." Noemi leaves me with the tall guy as she heads for the lady's room. When she returns, she says your little friend over there with the guy from the band shouted out, "I love ya" as I walked past him.

"Girl, he is crazy."

"Yeah, he probably is."

She sees my disappointment and says, "awe Nicole, you're upset about that."

"He was just being silly."

"Girl, I don't care. He really does look familiar though."

"Well, you should say something to him."

"Maybe later, I just want to enjoy the music." As we get ready to leave, I address the interesting mystery man. There was something familiar in his eyes and that voice. I ask him if we knew each other, maybe from school or job.

He laughs, "Oh, I thought maybe we had kids together. Did we sleep together?"

"Funny, I don't think so." I retort.

"Come on Noemi, let's go." Later that evening, I kept thinking I know that fool from somewhere. "Did I sleep with him? Humph. He wished I had. He would've remembered if I had." I'm in my bed and I get a weird text on my phone. It read, "Were you out listening to jazz tonight?" I'm freaking out, now. Someone is watching me.

I quickly text back, "Who is this?"

They respond, "We will talk tomorrow get yourself some rest." I call the number and there is no answer. The next day at work, I call until I get an answer. He still doesn't surrender, but that voice sounds so familiar.

"Look if you have dinner with me I will reveal myself."

"No, how about you tell me who you are and I will think about going to dinner with you?"

He laughs and then says, "I will soon tell you, just calm down."

I hung up the phone and "BAM", I got it. I jumped out of my seat and yelled, "Greg, that's who that was. Oh, that is too funny." I truly dismissed him from my phone and obviously my mind too. How could have missed that baritone voice? His voice was so descript. We talk later and I toy with him and finally reveal to him that I know who he is. Greg seemed pretty interested this time around. Every day, he was asking to see me. I felt like a little kid in a candy store. I lit up like a Christmas tree at the thought of hooking up with him every chance I could. Our relationship took off like a shooting bullet. What can I say, Greg had game. We dined together nightly, causing me to rush home from work to help the boys with homework and throw together a meal before heading out to be with him. I enjoyed the ride, but literally this man could not be contained or stay put. It was as if he'd been caged and appeared to be a wild animal set free. I am so accustomed to spoiling a man that I fall for. Not this one.

"Honey, your money is no good with me." What? Since when? Never been with a man that didn't like being spoiled, too. He wouldn't even let me cook for him. I managed to slip him some gifts for Christmas even though he wasn't big on Christmas because he felt it was just so commercialized with people spending abundantly and not recognizing the most precious things in life like simply spending time around one another. It was the least I could do. The man bought me flowers and shoes. You know how we, women are about shoes. Can you imagine a man that says all the right things and takes charge and you don't even realize you've relinquished your rights. Well, if there'd been any it was Greg. Brother had my nose wide open. After a while, I started feeling a little negligent with my two little men. They never reacted, but seemed to me that their bed times got a little later and homework wasn't displaying the same quality that it once had. As my first priority, I knew it was time to bring my three month excitement to the homestead or forfeit all that I'd been striving for to beat the dead beat dad replica in my little men to be. My children are my life first and foremost and if I can't be Greg's party girl then, I guess I will have to accept that. You see, Greg and I would not only go out to dinner, but sometimes divulge in nightly entertainment at a local bar for more adult conversation and music. We'd listen to live bands together or simply meet out with some of his friends. Whatever the case, we were always together. When I brought Greg around he was nervous because dating a woman with children wasn't his thing. Of course, my children are a lot like their mom and will give you a chance if they see that no harm is being done to me. My sons seemed to really like Greg. Greg suggested taking them out to dinner so that he could ease into conversation with them. My oldest loved it. He felt comfortable for once expressing his likes for the female gender. Every weekend my sons and I go to the show as a family outing and Greg gladly joined us. The boys were extremely happy to have a man accompanying us. He even invited us to partake in his childhood pass time of skating. My boys weren't skaters and neither was I, but we welcomed the idea anyway. Later, the pompous one decided, we all needed new skates if we were going to be rolling with him. Greg bought us skates and the boys were truly grateful to have him aboard. Everything seemed to be going so smooth between Greg and me. He'd mentioned a couple of times that he never wanted kids and he loved not having to be responsible for the lives of others. I figured he was speaking of a woman wishing to have kids. He'd already involved himself with mine so I truly wouldn't detect a problem with what we had fired up. After much love expressed, time spent and approximately two months later Greg began to distance himself. He would send text messages and refuse to see me. I didn't understand. I was lost. Devastated and without a clue as to why. I think this one broke all hell loose. I found myself looking for him at places we'd made our own. I engaged in numerous conversations with his friend Rosco. No matter what my plea, he refused to answer or see me. Now, being rational would have worked better with me. The old honesty approach, "Baby, I'm not a daddy and I really only want time with you. The whole kid thing is starting to bore me." *But no...* He had to just up and coward out on me. I think I may have snapped. I found myself online finding all properties affiliated with him whether it was through his mama, brother, sister, uncle or whoever I could find, the brother was going to hear my wrath. I jumped in my little Toyota and drove to his home only to not quite make it there at all. "No… this can't be happening to me." My car engine had literally locked up on me on the other side of town. "Oh My

God, this must be a sign from you to leave his selfish behind alone." Boy how I hated his ass this very moment. I thought to myself, *I do not wish to hear from him at this point, now that I've made a complete fool of myself chasing someone that does not want to be with me.* I realized that just because someone treats you special do not mean that they won't leave you. My children adored him. What a disaster. After this experience I found myself in a dark place. I was hurt. I recall the feelings of bliss.

***

A Cancer Man

I never imagined liking a soul such as yours… you're unique in character and seemingly somehow sweet… now don't misunderstand me you're a handful for sure…your stubborn and resistant in complying to my quizzing nature…I fret and get upset but can't seem to place you in a category with the rest…with this ongoing laid back pace, you cause me to find my place… It does not get to empower or embark on your taken space… you redirect me from my negative nay says and push constantly forward, letting me know you've got the gist of it and I'm not being simply ignored… I like your handle its quite different from before…there's something different about you that I liked the moment I stepped through your door…I'm determined to know you and get to your core… there's an intrigue you've inspired in me that simply wants to have more…before I met you I felt as if I'd let my heart become tore…Healing is a process and your slow and with ease pace you're feeding me is heavenly to my taste… so often I want to know everything up front ,but sweetie you position me steady and only reveal to me when you are ready…there's something mystical or obscure that has me taken by such lure… I fantasize with thoughts of you in mind…hoping that this patience instilled will be well worth our time…I'm attracted to your confidence and such manly display, hoping and wishing nothing leads you astray…your possibly puzzled, even uncertain of what kind of woman I am ,but know that I am capable of handling you and pleasing you in every which way…I am a gem that glistens and makes your heart listen…treat me with honor, respect, and admiration and I will shower your with true affirmation…You're strong, secure, and carry an aura of your own, you are that man I'd never thought I'd give the chance to be known…I embrace your energy and hope to see this through for I've sought out many 'til there time was overdue….I see potential in you and find myself determined to stay in the game, desiring that your mind will say the same.

***

Eight months go by and I'm content and ok with being alone. At this point, I know that I'm not the typical woman out here that will fall head over hills for most male types. He must be able to tap into my intellect. A conversation and personality flies high with me. However, with time alone my heart has numbed and rested for months. I find myself busying around the outside of my home, retrieving trash from the lawn, when I spot a handsome man smiling at me. I smile back and think to myself, "Oh boy, what's his story?" The man appears to be leaving the hardware store in eye's distance of my home. He pulls up and extends a compliment. We began talking and never remove the smiles from our faces. I ask him what his status was. He replies, "I'm divorced and single."

"Oh wow, really? How is that so?"

"I just haven't remarried."

"Is there a girlfriend?"

"Well, I've been seeing someone for close to two years, but I'm not going to marry her."

"So state your business. Are you trying to explore your options?"

"Of course I am, wouldn't be talking to you and trying to get your number if I wasn't. Is it ok for me to call you?"

"Hmm, I guess I could give you my number."

"What's your name?"

"Nicole and you are?"

"It's Orlando."

"That's different. Well, I guess I will be talking to you, Mr. Orlando."

"Ok, stay sweet." I smile and head towards my porch. Orlando called that same evening and we talked for quite some time. He really seemed nice. Since the day we'd met, we talked several times a day. I'd been to his home and he'd visited mine. Dating was far and few. He preferred buying things for me rather than ordinary dating that couples were accustomed to. I had many ideas about that, but he assured me that he was really feeling me and desired to be with me solely. Periodically, I questioned the relationship prior to us and never quite received the confirmation of it ending. I could only account for the way he'd been treating me. As time went on so did the pressure of me wanting confirmed closure of he and the never mentioned woman. As my mother always said, what's done in the dark will soon come to light. I started feeling like things he'd do for me was out of guilt and keeping me clouded. On Sweetest Day, Orlando comes to visit me and brings me a non-thoughtful, monetary gift and his phone is constantly blowing up with calls. He seems anxious and scurries out the door of my home. He tells me he will call me later. I'm annoyed and decide to call him for answers. He explains that he will tell me everything later. At this point, all hell has broken loose once again in my life. The woman he'd been seeing has found out about us. He tells me he feels so bad, but has to reveal a truth to me. "I've been with this woman since my divorce 10 years ago. My mouth is gaped open and I am appalled. Once everything dies down, a couple of days later he tells me, "I've always been in a relationship because I married young and went right into another relationship. The woman I was seeing and I have broken up because this isn't the first time I've cheated on her, but everything I've told you about loving you and wanting to be with you was true. I just need some time to myself to be alone and see what it's like to be single. I know we will probably end up together, but I just don't want to be in a committed relationship so soon. I want to be ready and right by you."

"This fool is trying to shelf me." For those sistahs out there that don't know what "Shelving" means, I'm going to break it down for you. To shelf someone is to place them in a possible option category or view after exhausting other options at a later time. You see, you think you have something good, but there just might be something that you might enjoy or desire even more. So to shelf one is to put them through a whole lot of shenanigans and lies to keep them staying put and still with hope, while they, your lover or partner can sow his wild oats, venture on with single finds and once exhausted and still no new perfect mate, return back to you. The problem is they will continue to look for prey and if they felt you weren't the total package in the beginning they will continue to return to you when others fail to intrigue them. Being put on the shelf is not a pretty picture. I've seen so many friends waiting on their guy to simply choose them while he moves on seeking something else. Wow, from Greg and now, Orlando eight months later.

"Orlando, you should've been honest in the first place instead of embedding false hope in this thing we had going. You are now, simply a labeled liar in my eyes. Ten years is another marriage and as far as waiting around for you, that I will not. I won't be a second guess for you because I can do better than, I think I want to be with you or I'm pretty sure, but need time to think. You take all the time you need and I will continue to move forward without you. You've done nothing more than lied and portrayed someone you are not." Short and not as hurtful as the last. Four months and once again I'm done. Orlando continues to call and check on me and offer his services or help with whatever I may need and I assure him I will be fine. I recall how excited I was when I'd met Orlando.

***

A Pisces Man

Is it me or have all rules ceased upon the mere presence of he......he comes about full of joy with a smile no woman can ignore...... no pout or scowl on his face awaiting admiration's return so he can learn his place......as he glance at my beauty by chance could it be…the clear image of a brother so handsome and attracted to me......he's charming and honest with female baggage assured, the question is has he yet to be lured… it's a risk ,but he toys with regrets of dismiss, his eyes marvel with hers of thoughts of their very first kiss…yielding to thoughts of something understood…he wonders if his desires and fantasies would ever fair to that of good… pursuit is in question, but far gone is thy mind…wishing and acting, playing role after role, seeking and blending with every inch of her soul…something is majestic… each feels it in the air…stopping this communication, one wouldn't dare…I feel no emptiness, he's robbed it in the mist of my despair…the moment I looked into him, I knew it would be there…the sense of his beauty which mirrored in his glare…how innocent, while of age to take back the old feelings of center stage…unleash the sentiments of two engaged and break away from life's lonely cage and explore life with one so, you and hope time will prove him too be true......seeking him not only in bliss, but down times as they may exist…adoring him continuous, and answering his many requests while seeing temptation at its defeat and beaten by the very best......search within the big heart of thee and travel through time to see, that the underlying heartbeat is the harmonious music of you and maybe he.

***

It's the holiday season and it's been a couple of months since Orlando. I'm still bitter from the series of events stripping me from my fairytale of love, but who wants to be alone during the holidays? I'm actually too busy to be proactive with my love life concerns right now because my life has become consumed with basketball. My youngest son, Kendall is now delighted and entertained by the notion of playing basketball for his school's team. I am hustling my butt on the regular, Tuesday, Friday and the entire weekend. As team mom, I'm assuming all parents remember to bring snacks for the games. I actually love the excitement seen in my youngest son as he attempts the game. My sons have never wanted to stick through anything, but this was his call and I, too am enjoying the ride. The social pact formed among the parents is really cool. We scream and holler at the plays worse than the children. Although my son is not experienced, he has the desire to be involved and that's enough for me. I'm spreading myself thin because the oldest is becoming envious and I've got to cultivate that one in activities as well. He has joined so many things in school this year in high school and won't commit to any of them. I find myself picking him up every other day from staying after school looking for his niche. My oldest, Brenton has always hated sport's activities, but feels left out now that the youngest is enduring a path of his own and no longer wishing to only follow the shadow of his big brother. My oldest son is an artist with great creativity, imagination and all the potential needed to become a great artist. I wreck my brain for ideas to entertain him and suddenly, I've got it. My birthday is around the corner and he must create a masterpiece just for me. I clear my schedule on a non-basketball day for Kendall and take my sons to the arts and crafts store. We purchase an easel and paint colors with brushes and head home. Brenton is ecstatic. I think to myself, *Way to go mom.* In the meantime, I'm feeling a friend intervention night in need. A couple of my female and male friends meet out for a night of cocktails and jazz. We are engaging and having a ball. A woman approaches us with a flyer for a Speed Dating event. We are joyful and silly at this point and asking the lady all kinds of questions. She smiles and encourages us to support her event. We all agree that the idea sounds inviting, although a couple of us at the table were married and definitely not going to attend. The funny thing is all of my friends turn to me and chant, "Go Cupid, Go Cupid." I laughed and thought to myself just maybe. The evening with friends ended and as I headed for home I thought more and more about trying this Speed Dating event. My logic was that one day I will develop a dating organization of my own and this would be another useful experience to add to my data.

Two weeks later, I find myself at a quaint little café where the Speed Dating event was scheduled to take place. "Wow, there are a lot of females here. Where are the men?" The organizer of the event that invited me looks worried and says, "They will show. They've signed up and paid." An hour rolls by and they decide to begin. As I see it the men are either invisible or they are standing us up. The organizer seats three older gentlemen and one young at tables by themselves. She then, explains the format of the event. "Ladies we have four lucky gentlemen because the others that confirmed seem to have gotten lost. I will call you in fours and once the music stops so must your conversation. You will continue to visit each table until you have spoken briefly to each participating male and then, I will continue until all tables have met. Take notes for each seating and write whether you have interest in the person you spoke to. If we come across a match for the male and female they will be notified within twenty-four hours. Good Luck." This should be interesting even though I see nothing of interest here for me accept the Organizer's cute younger brother that seems to be in my age range. I actually had the opportunity of chatting with him earlier with one of the two drink tickets. He was cute, endearing, but not quite my type. No kids. My first table is with a gentleman that seemed scorned from his past. He began telling me about his two ex-wives and how they felt he showed no emotion. He expressed having a temper at a young age and maturing as he got older. "Why would women want me to explode? I figure if they couldn't accept me for the way I was then, I don't need to waste my time with them."

He rattled on and on about the women of his past and before I knew it our time was up and he didn't know a darn thing about me. At table two sat a very heavy man. He was the big mouth type. Bragging and boasting about his business and what he had to offer a woman. "If she plays her cards right she may even win me over."

"Wow, I sure hope you find what it is that you are looking for." I couldn't wait for the music to stop. Table three was just my type entertaining and full of life, but twenty years too young. He was an adorable little chocolate, talker just like I like. My last table had an interesting guy. I believe he and I would have hit it off as well, but a woman that I'd been casually talking to while things were still being put together said she'd dated him years ago and they still talk. He was a little too old as well. His jovial spirit is what I liked. We talked about ourselves and he expressed how he'd been talked into this event at the last minute, but enjoyed having women come to the table just to meet with him. "I wouldn't do it again, though. I believe in meeting a woman the old fashion way. The evening dwindled with small talk and dancing among the remaining crowd it wasn't what I'd expected, but all is well. The organizer and I really hit it off and shared thoughts on her next event. I left with promises of keeping in touch. My thought on Speed Dating is men will not show. Has to be something in it for them to make it less pressured. Sports and mingle would definitely work. I will keep that idea for myself if I'm ever to start up a dating organization of my own.

***

Damaged Goods

I am at a loss for words, I feel empty inside…something's, missing and my world has subsided…the bliss I once had is now a tormented pass…It's a blur, a memory, a simple mist on the glass…sometimes I wonder why I must struggle with my heart's urge to love…am I to harden and become cold and dismiss every love story told… do I change or stay the same or find everyone to blame and risk dismay forever more or shut down my emotions allowing no man to ever score… I feel bitter and numb and see oncoming propositions as scum… I've become damaged goods, for my aching heart has become tart, and beginning anew, feels hopeless because I wouldn't know where to start… trusting, how easy it used to be, now skeptical of all brothers that have the audacity to step to me… So afraid to take a chance on something that just might be…uncertain whether meant to be alone or united with someone to accompany me… yet, still awaiting the chance, that one of life wonders may be, the perfect image of a man made so perfect for me.

Chapter Seven
The Males' Perspective

It never really dawned on me that there are two sides to every story in terms of my evidence presented of the horrid date scene. Men have concerns and issues as well. Although, it truly seems to be so much easier for them to meet new mates, the truth is sometimes it has been just as difficult as it has for us. The thing is with all of the meets and dating experiences I have had, I have collected a few new friends of the opposite gender on my continuous journey. When speaking to them they can actually rationalize the reasons they act in the manner in which they do. Patrick, an old friend of mine, makes no bones about it. If a woman does not respect herself why should he? I expressed how harsh that statement sound, but had to agree that if he did try to give respect it may not have been appreciated or the woman may not have been receptive. If a woman is taught or simply shown that the little hole between her legs is her money maker than she is also taught to use it at her disposal. Patrick expresses that this is how the friends with benefits thing actually started and this is why it has been so hard for women to get the total package from men these days. "Why put up with conforming to all the things you want from a man if we can simply pay a little something for a little something from a willing participant." In other words, if I can pay for your hair, nails or even a bill and receive benefits without investing my time dating and getting to know you, than why not go for what's been made an easier approach to getting the ultimate goal that men hunt after most. It truly hurts me to feel like this is what it comes down to. So many men out here agree that dating a woman and getting to know her takes too much effort. Even a friend of mine has told me that I simply want too much and that I am unrealistic for desiring to be dated. Old school men know better than this, but apparently there are yet, still a few of them that has converted to the new age mindset that dating can be omitted. I contribute this factor to women not showing the much needed respect for their selves. Many women have adapted the male attitude in order to hide their hurt from being hurt. I've heard sistahs say I'ma get mine even if he decides he isn't going to be with me, he will pay for this. It's like justification for giving up their goods to someone that they don't expect to be right by them, but feeling pacified by gifts or deeds done to say that one didn't get over on them. There's always those guys that feel like with all the women out here that hold tight to their under garments there are always going to be those that don't. Of course, who wants a man that has no respect for his self and would sleep with anything? I've expressed to my friend, Patrick that this is probably why I tend to gravitate to older males. I believe that many of them hold true to old fashion beliefs and still believe in getting to know a woman before getting with that woman intimately. Of course there are some old fools still out there, but many are more reserved and content with having them a lady that is theirs.

Patrick looks at me and laughs, "Nicole, baby, you have to understand that this is not personal. A man will sleep with a woman given time and opportunity. I don't care how old we get, we still want your panties."

"That is ignorant, Patrick."

"I know, Nicole, but women are not making it hard for us any longer. I've told women on several occasions that I am married and they still have the nerve to ask am I happy?"

"Yeah, I suppose you have a point, but just because it's easy don't mean it's good for you."

"Men have different mindsets from women, but you all out here not respecting yourselves are making it very hard for decent men to resist."

Curtis, another good friend says women are always trying to get over on good brothers. "Nicole, how about I do over and above when it comes to treating a woman special. When I'm just getting to know a woman, I ask her where she would like to meet out for a first date, I show up with flowers. I mean the whole nine yards."

"Ok, then, what seems to be the problem? You should have met the perfect match by now with that kind of chivalry."

"Sure, if I'm looking for a gold digger type. The last women I met requested every meeting take place at a pricey restaurant and after several dates, she still had not offered to do anything in regards to appeasing me. She never offered to cook or even make me a sandwich."

"Wow."

"I feel that you are a nice girl, Nicole, but a lot of these women out here are just as bad as the stereotypical male. They are out here simply to see what they can get. This is why I don't start off dating a woman with dates. I rather talk to her a number of times to see where her head is at first. Besides, I've since then learned that coffee dates are probably more appropriate for initial contact dates."

"Yeah, I would've suggested a simple donut or bagel shop as a first meeting as well."

Curtis continued to rattle on and on about women that were out for everything from a man's money, dating privileges, handyman services and whatever else they believe they can manage to get for free from a man. He talked about women with well to do jobs that cried broke every week as if to put themselves on an allowance plan with a man. My mouth gaped open as I attentively listened to this man's horror. He had definitely been burnt by the female gender. He would need a very understanding partner to see him through a positive experience of dating. Curtis now, sees a woman that he has no intentions of committing too that requires very little of him. My question is how fair is this to the woman that receives him with no expectations? I would venture to say her self-esteem may not be up to par. It's funny because I think of the speech I give to my young men. I tell them that the woman they meet should be able to pay her own bills. You as a gentlemen are to date her and spend time getting to know her. If you are not staying with these women then there is no reason you should be paying their rent. If after time has been invested and trust established you feel the desire to help her with things down the road because of the time spent with her cooking and catering to you, then so be it ,but your responsibility is to date and get to know her not take care of her financially. These are girlfriends not, wives.

Men that have been scorn in their marriages see things differently from the males that have had positive relationship experiences. My close male friend Randy simply adored his wife. However, once the reality of his situation was understood he turned from such the great catch to bitterness over due. Randy had a wife that did everything under the son known to be morally wrong to him. It is usually the male in the relationship showing out and acting a fool, but not this time. My friend, Randy has vowed never to marry again after the experience of his ex-wife Keisha. He feels that women are manipulative creatures put on earth to sway the thought process of men. He loved Keisha so much. Keisha on the other hand felt he was a mediocre lover, not so attractive, but financially the man in her plan. I was cool with Keisha as well, but my heart went out to her husband because he truly wanted things to work with her in spite of her worldly ways. He saw her being in every man's face as flirty, but innocent. Unfortunately, his boys knew the truth and many questioned him about it and he'd simply reply, "Keisha is just being, Keisha." There wasn't anything he wouldn't do for her. She spent all of his money and never stayed home. Other friends commented that she wasn't even sleeping with him regularly. We attended a mutual friend's wedding and she was seen throughout the night strutting around with several of the groom's men. Randy believed every lie Keisha told and all of her dramatic calls for attention were accepted. Randy was definitely not eye candy, but he was so cool and truly likable. I knew plenty of women that would have been happy to have him. Of course, Keisha ruined that. He will not be good for another woman in this life time. Keisha met some no good brother and began spending more and more time with him and less and less time at home. One of Randy's friends decided it was time for him to wake up and smell the coffee. He saw Keisha out at a popular spot with the no good brother she'd been hanging out with and phoned Randy immediately requesting his company for drinks. He sat in a discreet area and waited for Randy to show. Upon Randy's arrival, nothing seemed out of the ordinary until Randy spotted Keisha nuzzling on the ear of the unfamiliar man. All hell broke out and of course that was the end of Mr. Nice Guy. Randy has never been the same since this. Keisha didn't know what hit her as she fell her tramp ass right out of her seat. Randy had played the nonchalant fool for way to long. The wife we all knew as tramp, whore and gold digger was now, history. Problem is Randy couldn't find the trust in women anymore and as a result, women weren't able to get to know the good he once represented.

Kyle my neighbor is quite the philandering one and enjoys the chase. Periodically, we engage in a little one on one update of our lives, the children and our single status. He expresses that he has been with all kinds of women and that they are all out here naïve. He expresses that when a man tells a woman something she should listen and stop trying to read more into it then there is.

He states that he is up front at the beginning. I tell them, "I like my life just the way it is, without the hassle. If I wanted to hear nagging all day long I would have stayed married. I can have a good woman if I wanted too, but the truth is I don't want to settle down and I don't feel like doing right." Now, I will say that the brother is quite street flashy, well employed and simply downright disrespectful at times when it comes to women ,but for some reason he seems to keep them coming left and right by the bus loads. My girlfriend and he caught each other's eyes once and I tried to give her a hint that he was in player mode, but she didn't listen and found herself highly disappointed. He's your typical, wanting to be cool fool running around here trying to land as many pieces of ass that he can. Beware. The moral of his story is women know what they are getting into when a man tells them how it's going down from the start. Kyle exclaims that his lifestyle is simply at ease. He has no reason to lie to a woman because it's more women out here than men and he can pick and choose as he wishes. He says that someday he will settle down with a gem, but for now he is going to splurge among the female population a little longer. I can't say much because you can see straight through his kind and if females out here don't see what I see shame on them. All I can do is sit among the elders in the neighborhood and shake my head at his immature behind.

Alex is a very good friend of mine, but he is very unrealistic. He is what I like to call the typical momma's boy. No woman is ever going to be good enough unless they meet all of his momma's stats. Alex says he doesn't need a woman for anything more than a good lay. I was appalled when he said this.

"Wait Sis, don't be angry with me. All I'm saying is that women don't cook or clean anymore, they all professing doing their own thing. Moms still looks out for a brother. I can take my laundry to mom and she will take care of it for me. Whereas you ask a sister and she's screaming, she ain't nobody's maid. I mean, it sound worse than it is, mom is still cooking all my favorites and here this sister just wants someone to treat her out. How do I know if she even knows how to cook or clean? We, men are simple creatures, beer, food and sex."

"Yeah, so much for companionship. You need to get off of your mom's milk and fend for yourself even if you choose not to connect with a woman. There is no reason why a grown ass man takes his laundry to his mom's place. Oh, and by the way this is not cave man days, get your own damn beer."

"Nicole, you don't get it."

"Oh, yes I do, your mother has disabled you from being a great man to a much needed woman out here by spoiling your dirty behind and still treating you like a two year old."

"Maybe so, but these women out here aren't ready to sit down and be there for their men."

"Are you saying that women are too independent or no longer have time for a man's needs?"

"I'm just saying the old fashion type woman is kicked to the curb and these women out here now, well, they are satisfied with whatever. The ground rules have changed. You use to could meet a nice girl and marry her, but now these superficial chicks out here are not homebound."

"Wow that is funny because I sense that the men today aren't really looking for the old fashion, good girl types anymore."

The more and more I listen to men retort about the women out here and their experiences, the more and more I realize that dating can be just as difficult for some of them as well.

After hearing my male friends vent about women, I suppose I understand some of the foolishness I encounter out here. It sounds like finding a decent woman can be just as much of a challenge for men. Men are suggesting the non-respect for women is because women are not displaying themselves to be respect worthy. How interesting. Men suggest that they no longer have to play by all the rules to get the goods. They express that women will give it up for as little as a chocolate shake these days. Men that are scorn simply look at us as if we all are up to no good. Poor, Poor Momma's boys just can't give up that breast milk for store bought. It's nothing like momma and the women aren't cutting the chase these days. One of my male friends says women no longer need men.

"We just get in where we fit in." I looked at him perplexed and he explained that things have been different in the date scene ever since women start passing up men in the work place. "Women became the dominant figures in relationships and the aggressors. A lot of men out here are just simply not having it."

"Wow!" I couldn't say anything because as old fashion and ole school as I'd like to believe I am, I did portray the more dominant role when it came to decisions and finance because of my more positive financial status. As I began to bite my lip and look guilty, my friend, Gary expresses that he knows that he has just described my role as a wife in my former marriage to Brandon. It took a long time for someone to show me my place as a woman after being married to Brandon for ten years. All I knew was to take charge. As I find my wants and address my concerns, I pray that whomever I meet will have similar interests, understanding and a background mirroring mine.

Chapter Eight
Historical Data Explains It All

My ultimate life style before now would have entailed a man with the potential to love me unconditional and be a mentor to my sons. I wanted to know that I could put my life back together again after divorce. I'd watched my husband of ten years start anew and slip someone right into the empty space I'd left, so easily. My children had become convinced that all of my relationships had ended because of me being too hard on men. They often referred to their dad as being correct about me not being easy to deal with. I felt bad that they couldn't understand, but assured them that if I didn't stay with someone it was because we weren't a fit for each other. I feel like the guy I settle with has to be a fit for me and also, a match for my boys. Although deep down inside, I know that my children will like whoever their mother likes. It would be a plus if the man has experience with kids. It takes a special kind of individual to come into something new and open up to someone else's children. My children need to feel that whoever comes into my life has my best interest in mind. They simply want me stable as they see their dad.

Once my oldest retorted, "Can't you see we need men in our lives." I truly felt as if someone had cut me. It became unknowing pressure to give my sons a father figure. Although I often pride myself in the fact that I am primarily raising two boys alone, I knew that they lacked male guidance. I'd tried everything to assure that their mental health was in good standing. They'd been involved in male mentoring groups, sports and even social worker's groups after my divorce. After seeing the disappointments in their faces each time things didn't work in my relationships or simply the letdown hopes from a bad date, I became more and more reluctant about bringing men I dated home. I wanted to avoid them getting close to anyone that may not persist in our lives for the long haul.

All I ever wanted was the romantic fantasy to come alive. I felt that just because my first marriage was terminated, it didn't mean that I wasn't to meet my true love and live happily ever after. I know that there are plenty of women in the world seeking to have their Mr. Right, but I had faith that it was destined to happen for me. Girls like me didn't just settle for eternal single life styles. I am destined to be with a mate of my choice. At least that was the belief that led my life in circles of the hopeless romantic thus far.

I held true to my dreams and desires. I measured the worth and compatibility with every man I dated. I wished for the escort to the weddings, the companion to try new things with, a travel mate to attend exotic excursions with me and someone to embellish the romance in me. When I get sick and feel down, I want him to be there to hold me. During a movie hour on the sofa, I wish to curl up beside him. In those unexpected moments when my body becomes squirmy and the need to be touched arises, I want the man I've bonded with to satisfy all of my intimate needs and sexual urges. The funny thing is that I've always had me a special someone and now, being alone seems invigorating compared to the let downs I've encountered preceding the years of my divorce. Most have fallen short of the dream man I've conjured up in my mind.

At this time, I am cleansing my body and mind. I constantly remind myself that the process of being alone is healthy for my spirit. I've masked myself and persistently pushed forward. The love of my children sustains my sanity in worlds falling apart. Observing the many that mirror situations like my own, help me to realize that I'm not alone in the lonely hearts club. The great thing is that there isn't a contender or past suitor that marvels me any longer. I've made a pact with my heart that each beginning is new and never to be held accountable for past disappointments. It has also been a rule of thumb of mine; never to return to a relationship from the past. Now, I'm guilty of conversing with my exes when they call, but nothing happens beyond small talk and simply keeping things cordial. My heart recalls the stressors from each man of my past and rebels against releasing trust again.

As a little girl, I admired my parents so much. My dad was a good provider and truly in love with my mother. They began seeing each other while still in high school. Today, the world has advanced so much and times have changed, the likeliness of stumbling upon a mate that early is unlikely. My parents shared a success story all of their own. Two young people from a low economic area that aspired to do better and accomplished much more than was expected. My parents were one of two black home owners on the block that my siblings and I grew up on. They had a relationship built on love. Hurdles were dealt with and never caused them to astray. My dad never wanted to see my mom unhappy. My mother didn't want for anything. My mother cherished their relationship and softened my dad like never seen before. My parents had parties with friends for each celebrated occasion. Their friends marveled at the chemistry and lack of nonsense absent from their relationship. It was about them first and foremost. They loved and cared for my siblings and I ascertaining that we were given the things that they did without. Their desire for each other, cause them to keep their marriage fresh by frequent travels around the world. The older we got, the more frequent they traveled. Their love lasted a life time and never diminished. My parents were married forty years when my dad was taken by illness. Their thing was envied by many.

When I went to marital counseling prior to my divorce the counselor asked, "What was the relationship like between your parents?" She revealed to me that I had to have a mate that I respected like my father and pointed out that I clearly didn't respect the man I had married. I thought about my husband's upbringing and how he was raise in early years primarily by his mother whom had divorced his father. Clearly, he'd lacked the knowledge of what a responsible man was. His qualities were nothing like that of my father and couldn't be compared to the absent father he lost to divorce. People are taught hate just as they are taught to love and looking back on the relationships that followed my divorce it all explains itself as to why the relationships failed.

The first relationship with Rick failed because he'd gone down the same negative paths as did his single parent mother. He expressed that she hustled and later used drugs. Although, this was not true for his siblings there was still a negligent past and love lost. Rick often expressed he learned to hustle from his mother. He'd made it through teen years successfully, but later shared a lot of the same negatives of being consumed by the street life as his mother. Fortunately, he did recover from his major negatives, one being the use of criminal intent to get what he wanted and the use of drugs. However, the hustle in him remained with every relationship he possessed with women and playing me was a mistake he wasn't as fortunate to recover from. I moved on. After dating of Rick, I recalled my relationship with Disco.

Disco desired the love of his mother more than anything and struggled with the relationship with his mother stemming from childhood issues. He recalled his father raising him strict and a strong grandmother's love. Some of the neediness I encountered in our relationship was due to his need to be loved by a woman that possessed those nurturing qualities of a mother. Over time, this kind of relationship can become consuming and overbearing. I never wanted to take on the role of any man's mother. The attachment and needy behaviors persisted and I felt compelled to run.

John, my third contender after divorce was determined to do what he felt he lacked in his marriage. He was determined to be the best father he could be and avoid hurt at all cost. This in turn caused many issues in our relationship because his choice was to date and give every available moment to his children. He was unreasonable and didn't know how to keep a relationship because he had never identified with a successful one. His unbelievable need to be obsessed with his children and no time for partner play caused the relationship to stray. You must water your relationship like a plant if you expect it to grow. Reluctantly, I moved on for all of my needs were not being met.

When I think of jovial Greg, I think of religious differences in our backgrounds that may have caused some concern. He grew up with a non-traditional religion in a strict environment that caused many of his views to be crossed. Although it was embedded early on, he sought out for his own truths and freedom that caused friction with his family norms causing him to be resistant and withdrawn with females he encountered. He took off like a speeding bullet if love seemed to have an impact on him. Believing that it would once again have him contained and under the influence of someone other than himself. He consumed himself with being alone for fear of non-acceptance. Our issue is that he'd never commit. I had a deep love for him, but knew our ideals were on different pages.

Last, there was Orlando. Now, this brother was brought up by grandma with the iron fist and a laid back granddad. This is not unusual about children of today, but his negatives he has on the relationship factor is marrying his first love too soon, straight out of high school and landing a male dominated job with those known to display whorish tendencies. His problem was thinking that he missed something being tied down so soon in life. The old philosophy that the grass is greener on the other side. We couldn't make it because of his cheating abilities and warped since of relationships. I analyze relationships all the time. There isn't a perfect relationship out there, but there are compatible ones. All my adult life, I desired the love that I was most familiar, the type of love shared by my parents. I think back to the tribute given to them as they celebrated their thirty-fifth Wedding Anniversary…

***

A time of recollection of the many joys experienced through such a bond held between two…

A perfect chance to renew and celebrate a love that still holds true…

A splendid time to remember the old memories kept and treasured by both of you…

A tribute to the many blessings God has bestowed upon the two of you…

Beautiful Offspring and moderate prosperity, just to name a few…

A heritage built through many years of love and dedication only the two of you knew…

A grand toast to the grand couple of thirty-five years of bliss…

Shall your strong endurance pave a path of assurance to more of life's beautiful events.

Chapter Nine

Definition of Self

If I had to describe myself, the words; sensitive, compassionate, nurturing, respectful, loyal, sincere, thoughtful, emotional and quality would be the first words that come to mind. Of course there are flaws and things that may not be the best characteristics or traits to possess.

Many of my friends would describe me as bubbly and really cool to be around. I'm like Oprah and Ellen, everyone loves them. Maybe it's an Aquarius thing, but something causes people to gravitate to us. Now, don't get me wrong I do like time to myself and can't endure smothering after a while.

On the flip side, I like a mate that enjoys time with me and shows persistence in being a part of my world. My sentimental aura is nurturing and giving. I remember reading lyrics that the singer, Alicia Keyes had written and thinking, this artist has so much in common with the way I think. I looked her up on line and there it was another Aquarian woman. I know that it is forsaken to say such things in terms of zodiac stuff in given religions, but people must admit, there is some true similarities in personality traits of people born during similar times of year. My personality is one that has always been driven by emotions. I cry when watching movies on the romance channel and I love hooking up male and female friends. They've even nicknamed me "Cupid". There's this crazy need that I have to see people happy. I divulge my children with my love and all the pleasures that my pocket book can afford or shall I say all the things I wish for them to have within reason. The funny thing is that may be the biggest flaw that I possess. When I love, I love hard and those I love are treated royally. I think of how special each man I dated felt while with me. I left a little part of me with each of them.

Upon their arrival, I'd flourish them with a home cooked meal and a hot sexy vixen waiting to please them, trinkets in a basket with a special note to get them through the day as they depart from my home. There wasn't a problem they had that I wasn't earnest to repair. Always available to hear the telling of their day. I was content with just having my mate be with me whether it was going out or cozying in.

My must haves in a relationship are simple. I know that many people may struggle in life and fall on hard times, but I require that a man be first and foremost capable of taking care of himself before stepping to me. Brandon, my ex-husband has given me the experience that I do not wish to encounter again. Never do I wish to be with a man that must live off of me. Yes, I love to cater to the man I'm with, but I like for it to be my doing not his asking. So simply put, he must be stable. The second thing that must be prevalent is security. Knowing that this man has my back. When I look at him I see a love for Nicole. This man is about me and therefore, he won't jeopardize his incredible find. I feel safe and for sure that he is genuine. The last thing is communication. I love a man that can indulge in a good conversation about anything. I think about the talking that takes place at the beginning of a relationship that never wants to stop. If I need to vent his ear is open to hear and support. Romance is my angle. It would be nice if he had a romantic flair, but if not be open to the possibilities. My male friend that expressed, I desire too much is sadly mistaken. I have only just begun. My mate's most important attribute must be to know love. All the things I've spoke on wanting are easy to have if the person loves you unconditionally.

There were special things that drove me close to each of my mainstay relationships and those things are the same things I hope to obtain in one mate destined for my future. Although it sickens me to think of my ex-husband, I recall him having the best bedside manner for a sick gal. He washed, scrubbed and cared for my feet better than any pedicure service I'd received. While I carried his children, pampering was just one treat I looked forward, too. Brandon would cook for me and possess the most gentle and caring manner while nursing me back to health. I'd hate to think it had anything to do with my being his meal ticket. Actually, I believe he did it because somewhere in the mist of his trifling ideals, he can be a good hearted man. However, we all know that my ex-husband never really had it going on for long while we were together. So, it's not hard to question his motives.

The lack of keeping a job or innate male qualities of holding down the fort were often compromised. However, thinking positively, he would be a great companion if it was only based on the bedside manner alone.

Rick was street. I've never been with the so called cool guy. They've never had interest in me. Rick made me feel as if he had a handle on things no matter where we roamed. He'd had a lot of negative experiences, but had an inflated ego that not only empowered him, but forced everyone else to accept him. He brought fun and excitement into my family's life. He accepted me and my children from the start. He had a way with me and respected the non-ghetto, quirky, girl from the other side of the tracks, the nurturing and loving person that I was. He made me come out of my shell. He exposed my, "Sexy." I never felt hot for any man until I'd met Rick. He excited me and spoke my language. Whatever differences we had, the chemistry was overflowing. Even though he'd obviously grew up hood, my sons still liked him knowing that he was a different caliber from the men they'd been around. I truly cared for him ,but when it was all said and done, our different worlds was exactly what separated the love we shared from our reality. However, I credit him with revealing the passion within me.

Disco was truly adorable. He was like my very own King Kong. He loved me so much. I definitely felt that it was about me, but the kid thing wasn't the fit I was looking for among other things that I found not to be so compatible. Disco compared every woman to me. I was his top contender and that I loved about him. He wanted me with him as much as I could stand. Things were good, but I started to feel claustrophobic and like his love for me was more of an obsession. I loved his intent to have us pray together in order to assure we stayed together. I credit Disco with showing me how it feels to be put on a pedestal by someone that loves you and luring me back home to my spiritual base.

John reminded me of myself, being a financially secure and self-disciplined individual. He often referred to himself as being plain and ordinary. I loved his laid back demeanor. Definitely wasn't your male street molly like so many men. There was just something family feeling about him even though he'd never taken the initiative to connect with my sons. Maybe the feeling was more of a content man. When we were an item, I recall the comfort in knowing that I'd hear from him during his routine breaks throughout the day. Although I was second to his children, he initially compromised for me. I felt he did the minimal required to maintain our relationship. I credit him with showing me how compromising occurs when a person is truly feeling you. Of course, as relationships mature the openness to compromise tends to look bleak.

Now, Greg displayed the qualities of the closest thing to what I'd thought to be the perfect mate. He appeared to want to please me from the time we began dating throughout our time together. My children liked him a lot. There is something about a guy treating mom nicely that wins over the children. He had a lot of friends and even my friend, Noemi seemed to have taken a little too much of a liking to him. His personality spoke volumes. He had cool for sure. Greg made me feel special and he spoke my language. The only thing that concerned me was he seemed to have lacked bedside manner. He was determined to have me toughen up in instances like; illnesses or areas of weakness. It was as if time wouldn't permit me being down and out for too long of a duration because he needed his team player on point at all times. I felt like Tina in the Ike and Tina Story. No time for rest, got to keep things moving. His presence was powerful. It was like he had an aura that said he was above all bull. I felt like he was the man for me. I never doubted his feelings for me. He spoiled me with surprises and allowed me to simply be his woman.

I learned how to let go of all the control and allow my feminine side a chance to flourish once more. I'd always felt like the man in my marriage and for once I felt I'd found a man that was strong enough to catch me if I fell. The impact Greg left on my life will never be forgotten. I truly fell for him.

Orlando was truly unexpected, but gave off a feel of a wholesome good guy. He was a hard worker and had skills. These traits reminded me of my father. My father worked hard all of his life and often referred to himself as a "Jack of all trades." Every woman wants a handyman. Orlando worked a steady job and indulged in all sort of carpentry work in his spare time. He even fixed a couple of things around my home. He never hung out with the guys and never missed a day calling to say goodnight. He kept things simple and adored me just for being me. He found attraction in me even when I wasn't my best. He gave the feel of a down home fellah, simply content with having time with me. He had a sensitive side just like me. I learned that things didn't have to be extravagant or complex to have an effect on me. I liked the idea of keeping things in my life a little simplistic.

I believe that a lot about my personality scares men. They want the fun girl with no strings attached, the friend with benefits, the non-committal type and the one that is going to give them a run for their money. I am fun, but fun has limits when there are two young men looking to mom to show them the correct path in life. A man has to show his "A" game to me and the boys must see positive intentions for their mom. As far as commitment is concerned, there is no alternative to that. If a man desires to be with me on a serious level he will commit. Now, don't get me wrong I can raise a little hell myself, but with given reason. Men often think it is cute when a woman curse them out, check their phones and ride their coat tails. If they are looking for their mother at close to retirement age, good luck. I refuse to feel insecure to the point of harassing my mate on the regular. That is crazy. If I can't trust you then, we don't need to be together. If I have to berate you or control you to have you do right by me, you've got the wrong chic.

Part of my problem has been giving the men a sense of my wifey skills and showing all that I have to offer too soon. Instead of coaxing them into a productive relationship, I've presented them with the start, the finish and the dessert. I think Steve Harvey made that analogy to a woman that seemed so much like me. I am the woman that feels too much like a relationship. That "good girl" stamp is still on my forehead from elementary school. She's really nice, but you know. Never be fooled by the book's cover is what I say to that. Good Girls like to have fun, too. Again, as expressed previously, I want the loving relationship I grew up knowing. I tried breaking my mode a few times with refraining from being to giving or thoughtful in previous relationship and it was truly hard not to write a poem, give a card or buy something he liked. I have never mastered the art of mind games. I notice women of today are much more skilled at manipulating, being aggressive and more appealing to the imagination. My demure disposition just doesn't cut it anymore these days. My old fashion, girl next door attitude unleashed in the new age world is truly out of place. I remember my girlfriend telling me she'd landed this great guy by shunning his friend who'd been showing her interest and calling the man's friend to her table. As she'd began inquiry of him, he told her of his friend being interested and she told him that was too bad because she was more interested in him not his friend. They dated for a while until she pegged him as too boring. Gina, another friend gave her new husband a run for his money before they got married. She was one of those who'd conquered the dating of multiple people and still managed to maintain the interest of her husband while luring him on the committal or marital page as herself.

My mother's friend's story of how she'd met her husband was the most fascinating of all. Her putting the word out to all of her friends that she was throwing a birthday party and all being expected to bring a single male friend was brilliant. My friends offered to do the same, but of course things didn't pan out the same with my friends looking out for me. I recall my mom's friend, laughing as she said, "Let's just say three men lingered around and the last one to leave is the one I married."

I gasped, "Wow, how proactive and rewarding." I remember partying with my older sister once and spotting an interesting man. I shared with Tracy that I'd love to talk to him and I immediately shrugged the thought minutes after I made the statement. As I'd turned my attention back to some of our friends, I noticed my sister and the guy engaging in small talk and jokes. All is fair in single and finding love. I truly feel like everyone changed with the times or was given, "Wheaties" as a kid to make them more empowered. Every time I've stepped out of my comfort zone and approached a man it ended in embarrassment. I recall this guy looking at me as if he was caught totally by surprise as I handed him a business card and after all the mustered up courage he never called. It may be just me, but the building up of nerve to make a new acquaintance is quite frightening. It's almost explainable why men have taken a stand and no longer attempt come-ons. Of course, there are always the aggressive women that learned the old familiar male role of approaching desired prey.

So, again why risk being rejected and why not let the women approach us. Humph. Although at times, I've envied the woman with the aggressive edge, I know that simply being me is the only way that I will land the mate that is right for me. My personality is innate and can only be altered so much before the good of my core exposes itself. I am who I am, a tender at heart woman born an Aquarian.

***

The Aquarian Woman

She's eccentric, yet endearing and a delight to surround…delicate and sensitive yet, creative and intuitive bound…thought to be passive ,but when taunted, toyed and stepped upon will show forced empowerment galore…Very giving and caring for those close to heart, making certain in every effort to always do her part…Some may say frugal ,but responsible financially she's sure to be…Full of love and desire that have many fall for and simply gravitate to thee…Conscious and deliberate in being the best in her craft assuring her genuine persona is always something felt and to be seen in the aftermath. A great pleasure, a great find, many men fear to entwine…to for sure, to real and too much like that committal feel…always striving never to quit until true love and desire are measured and equipped…Simply a rare find or jewel, only to be treasured and tampered with by life's most ratifying man pool.

Chapter Ten

Embracing My Life and My Choices

After much thought and reevaluation of my life to current, I've decided to reflect on what's going well. A relationship is great, but I realize it will come when the time is right. I can't believe I'm actually quoting the thoughts of many. I use to resent people telling me that a good man was sure to come, just be patient. Everyone forgets how lonely and agitating it is to consistently meet, "Mr. Wrong." Once you find your special someone you suddenly forget what lonely days felt like. It's like a teacher telling a parent how to raise their kids, but the teacher has no children of her own. In order to give advice to someone it's only valid in my opinion if you've experience it for yourself. That's my view on those that have been married or in relationships for years, yet giving advice to the single.

However, I've grown a bit and I'm approaching a year without dating a serious contender. My children and I continue to maintain our closeness. Brenton is in high school and the youngest continues to keep me active with ongoing activities. Although they have a significant age difference, they get along great. We are in the mist of planning our next family vacation. We continue our weekend festivities of the occasional theater, dining out and perusing the malls. The mall is my place of peace aside from my frequent attendance to church. I realize as a sole parent and provider sometimes I need time away from everyone. My son's still find it cool to go to the mall with mom, but of course this is the cell phone era and they are released to wander alone. Church is peace within itself. No talking simply, getting your praise on. So therapeutic.

My other avenue is that of my friends. I have plenty of friends willing to take a break from their spouses, boyfriends, children and even their lonely selves. Jazz nights are still a popular alternative and meal dates with friends work as well. No matter what my fetish may be, time alone or hanging out with friends, I've positioned my outlets as need be. Many of my friends are surprised in the lack of relationship talk. I've also refrained from putting friends with other friends and playing cupid altogether.

I've began to get into myself with changes in my diet and incorporating exercise. That new Latin dance DVD is so much fun. I won't lie it's still hard to stay consistent with my exercise and tend to my children and household after work, but the effort is there. My focal point of a relationship is no longer my priority. I'm sure there are great men out in the world seeking great women, but after looking back at my past and the energy invested, I could have been accomplishing other things that I've wished to experience or complete. Every month I have planned to step more and more out of the box. By the month of May, I plan to take golf lessons.

Over the summer maybe I will learn to speak Spanish language fluently. My friends all think I'm crazy with all of my goals and aspirations, but I believe that I am truly embracing my life for me. I realize that it is a choice to dwell on things you can't change or move forward and enjoy the blessings you have as you continue to enhance the quality of life that you have. One friend told me that she recall keeping busy as well when she was single. I'm not in denial. I'd love a companion, but I believe that being proactive in trying to meet the perfect one became discouraging and draining. My life is routine yet, open for new. Eventually someone special will come my way. In the meantime, I am living, breathing and putting effort in something meaningful, my sons and myself. Of course, some old habits are hard to break. Four out of the five men I've dated after marriage and even some meets placed in the friend zone still call to check on me. Many friends don't understand how bitterness has not taken over and how I allow men of the past to still indulge in the pleasures of conversations with me, but the truth is it confirms what my close friend, Diane and I believe, if you are good to a person they will always remember and always find a way of staying connected. Although I befriend exes I don't take it beyond that point. Friendship is as good as it gets. If ever I think to stray back down memory lane, something is said or done to remind me of why going back into past relationships is still a "Negative." The one guy that still has a piece of my heart is Greg. Although he hurt me profusely by disappearing the moment it got too involved, I have never felt the chemistry shared between us with any of my other loves. The capability of friends, lovers and his displaying you as his number one prize during the time of our relationship. Hearing from him regularly still brings a hum to my heart and yet still, I recall the hurt that keeps me grounded with him. I know that if I am ever to have a great guy enter my life in the future, the ties I have with the exes would have to end. No man wishes to be placed in given situations where he'd have to be inferior to those that have dated his new find in the past.

My boys are young, but highly influenced by a woman's emotions. I must contain myself at all cost if not for me, then definitely for them. They yearn for me to have a companion for fear that they will move on and venture new things that may leave mother behind. My oldest has broken it down eloquently for me. I assure him with or without a man, I am strong and the choices I make may reflect upon them, but in no way does it stop me from embracing my life. A man is an asset to us he does not make the great that we are.

***

All About My Boys

The offspring of mine is truly divine…I live, breath and conquer to make sure that they are fine… no help from their sperm donor or former known father of thee…just a praying mom that sacrifices daily and unconditionally…the hope is that they will grow to know the nurture and love shed for thee in order to embrace life most vicariously…instilling the fear of God and the ultimate love from me are hopes of good men growing and standing tall for all to see… the mere image of their father and mirrors of me…mask the beauty shared once between him and me…surely not meant forever ,but no mistake you see…the presence of two young men set out to be…I wish for them utter happiness, good health and comfort with life choices near and far beyond ,but most of all I wish for the known fact of love to be enthralled…the love I carry in my heart for them is a love that only a mother can feel…I declare that their wellbeing and given direction is truly a mother's seal on the channeled life of that of her sons and their first true love to be revealed.

Chapter Eleven
Irritated and Disgruntled

I'm on the right track. Eating healthy, incorporating exercise and making it just fine without dating anyone. My son's seem happy and are both doing fine. Whew. Their trifling dad's absence doesn't seem to be affecting them as much, all is good. It's Saturday and I'm following through with my hair washing ritual and the phone rings.

"Hello, Nicole?"

"Yes."

"This is Dr. Tate's office."

"Ok, is there something wrong?"

"Well, Nicole it appears that you have endometrial matter or cells showing up in your pap smear results and according to your age that shouldn't be. You see, endometrial cells pass in younger women and it is rare of women in their late thirties or forties. We would like for you to follow up with your gynecologist regarding this matter. A referral from the primary doctor must accompany you. We will fax it over to the gynecologist office for you."

"Wow. Ok, thank you. I will make an appointment right away." Lord knows I don't look forward to visiting my gynecologist. I did my annual female exam with my primary doctor just to avoid that office, dag. Just seems like since thirty-five years of age, my doctor is always suggesting some female procedure. I'm truly afraid to complain.

"Oh, if we zap that little fibroid from there you will have lighter periods. Hey, if we freeze your uterus you will not only have light periods, they may go away altogether. It beats having a hysterectomy." I mean really. My gynecologist specializes in everything and I come through the office looking like a guinea pig ready for experimentation every time. Finally, I go for my appointment. I'm on ten and so glad to go get this misunderstanding over and done with. Of course, that would never be me. "Sorry, Nicole, but we will need to do a biopsy to assure that there is no cancer in a matter such as this."

"Are you serious?" This is crazy. Of course there is a follow up to the follow up. On my return visit, the doctor carefully exam my vagina and stumbles upon a lump or cyst that is causing all the problems. Now, we all know what that means, surgery. Really?! I'm devastated. Upon my wait for the scheduled dooms day, I find myself no longer enthused with my diet plan, exercise and definitely not the likes of a man. My gynecologist just so happens to be a very pompous, self-centered, egotistical male. I've stayed with him this long because he did both cesarean births for my sons. My positive spin on life is now anxious and irritated. Can't believe I've got to have surgery for a stupid cyst. I'm livid. My doctor had the nerve to suggest everything will be ok in six weeks. I'll be able to have sexual intercourse again. Really. Who says that?

I couldn't help but retort, "I'm Not Seeing Anyone."

So fricken insensitive. My ex boyfriends are all calling for no apparent reason other than thinking they're shelving me and my mind is miles away. I was finally at ease and feeling content and now, this.

My mother was a dear for taking time out of her busy schedule to accompany me to the hospital for my cyst removal surgery. I remember feeling more angry that I was going through this ordeal than afraid. When I woke up in the recovery room I recall the pain being excruciating. It was like someone had placed a bad tooth ache in my vagina on the left side. Humph. That wasn't what I was expecting at all. I figure today's technology would somehow have me pain free. So wrong. I didn't see my doctor after the surgery. I assumed that since there weren't any guidelines or restrictions other than do as you can, I would be able to return to my job in a couple of days. A couple of days turned in to a few weeks. I couldn't believe I was still experiencing pain. Finally, I go for a follow up appointment with my doctor three weeks after the surgery and he insists that he told me the recovery would be six weeks long. I attempt to go back to work without his approval and find myself right back at home watching HGTV. My mom and sister continued to bring food and whatever I needed. Friends visited and asked what the hell was keeping me down so long? I felt so weak for not being able to bounce back fast enough.

Of all the times I took a sabbatical from sexual activity, this had to have been the worst. If ever you are conversing with women it becomes apparent that vaginal procedures after a certain age are the norm.

We just don't talk about it until we hear someone say, "Girl, I had that. It'll be a piece of cake." I had heard every woman's story of fibroids to hysterectomies, over flooding of menstrual blood to hit or missed monthly displays. It's funny how there is so much knowledge out here in regards to people sharing, but many are taking their experiences to their graves. It actually reminds me of the friends you share with and those you don't. I recall telling a friend of my recent surgery and she questioned as if I'd done something wrong. Really, the nerve. It's like the friend that paints the perfect picture and image of her life and never shares a flaw. She might as well make believe that my life is perfect because I won't be sharing a tidbit of my life story with her either.

Of course, on the other hand there are your heartfelt friends that are giving the low down and hoping for any ear to listen or solution given to help them out of their current let down. All my life, I've been more of an open book because I find it therapeutic rather than sulking all alone. However, in recent years I find that some things you are just better off keeping to yourself. Expressing excitement to friends about a new date prospect is limited. They are now starting to think it could be me when things don't flourish. What a pity, don't they know by now I do no wrong? They don't seem to understand that finding a suitable mate takes time and sometimes it takes some longer than others. Kinda like this miserable recouping situation I'm finding myself in after surgery. I have to just hurry up and wait as my older sister always tells me. My friends have called a ton of times wondering why I'm still recovering and the patient ones seem to be my exes. It's like I've got new "Cookie" that awaits them. They call everyday wondering the status of my "Stuff" not realizing that the trauma that my vagina has been put through will make me even more selective in whom I choose to let indulge in it. They want to bring me something, take me out and even volunteer to rub my feet. The comments of how ripe it will be after the absence of activity and voicing their thoughts of how the peach is new and refreshed. Just out of their damned minds, I say. I can't see intimacy or passion past the throbbing pain. This vaginal tooth ache is irritating as hell.

Weeks go by and the pain has subsided. Once I felt better, I returned to work and things began to fall back in place. Now, I do wish I had a nice guy in my life to hold me and tell me everything is ok. I fight the notion of being lonely and pitiful and continue to work on my restoration process. Things are definitely feeling back to normal. All those past hounds don't have anything coming. My healed vagina is now my newest prized possession. The next man to enter this sanctuary is going to have to get on his knees and beg for it or shall I say be a very worthy servant.

I can now say, "I'm a soldier." Can't believe the pain and recovery is over. I was so miserable. I'm feeling so much like the old me. Now, this is what I'm talking about. Exes are still hopeful and I am so aloof of the intentions that they are putting forth. One, they had their chance and, two nothing has changed from dating them before. It's funny because I now, feel more so than prior to my surgery, that a man is the least of my concerns. I suddenly feel like trying something different like a new social atmosphere to spread my wings or maybe showing some gratitude for my regained health. A plan is definitely on the rise for a more, healthy lifestyle and that includes the selection of men that I consider. Lord knows they can deteriorate your health just from the stress they put you through.

Sometimes it takes an unexpected set back or situation to bring different thoughts into play. My health means a lot more to me than it did prior to my surgery. I believe it was a rude awakening for my sons and others that depend on me to make things happy. I realize that everything and everybody was more important to me than taking care of myself. I've spent numerous years in my life catering to the needs of others and now, I can honestly say I wish to cater to me now. My wants and desires are now a priority. I think that even though the surgery wasn't contributed to some wrong doing in my life, like eating the wrong things or lack of healthy preferences like smoking or something, it impact me so much just having to sit down and take it easy. All I can think about is how glad I am it wasn't Cancer. If ever there is one disease I fear, the big "C" is it. It took the one man that I identified as being just that, a man away from me.

My father was the only real example that I've ever had shown to me of what a man was supposed to consist of. The men I'm faced with today are nothing like him. My dad adored his wife and cared for the well-being of his children. He was a jack of all trades. He knew enough about it all. We didn't have a want for much. My parents were truly a match well made. My mother was a house wife for years and later entered the work place as a very productive citizen, making a lucrative income as well. However, it was never about the money, but the commitment shared between two people that showed their children that fairytales do exist.

Today, it's not about commitment. The display appears more like a scene from Friends with benefits. Men don't date like they use too. They fund things for women and come by from time to time to tap that thang. If that's all I'm offered I must decline. I want the fairytale. After being in a recouping situation for weeks I had a lot of time to think and unfortunately the truth is there is nothing impressing me among the men here in Chicago. The thing is that individuals are so sold on making things fit. Men as well as women are quick to assume that a situation will change just for them. He says, she is whorish, but once she get a hold of me she'll slow it down. She says, he doesn't wanna marry again, but after I put it on him and cook a few of my specialties he'll come to grips with the plan. I've been guilty of this mind set as well.

Truly it took Greg to bring me to my reality. Greg said clear as day, "Honey, I never wanted kids or the responsibility." He left a sistah hanging the moment those kids began getting too close or the moment it felt a little too much like family. Timing is everything and I've come to realize that the surgery was meant to sit my black behind down and force me into some reflecting time. I think after my long, drawn out recouping ordeal, I've come to the conclusion that I don't want to deal if it isn't appealing to my desires of a man. Sure, I will hear a brother out, but the moment I hear something that doesn't sound like a fit, I'm out. I don't wish to waste anymore of my time trying to force a fit or giving hope to a situation that is doomed from the start. At this point, I do not wish to waste a brother's time and nor do I wish for him to waste any of mine. I must admit, it would have been nice to have had a man in my life when things got a little rough for me. Aches, pains and all, I would have loved to have been hugged and told everything is alright and you will get through this. "I'm here for you, baby."

However, that wasn't the case and the more I think of it, the surgery experience simply made me even stronger than I've already been. Hell, raising two young men and staying financially strong isn't as easy as it looks. Momma is working this single parent thing out and end results shall prosper through my lil men. Funny thing is that after all the anxiety and recouping, I truly have been less hopeful of relationship stuff. I don't know what's going on with me, but just don't feel these men out here are worthy any longer. It seems like the more estranged I've become from the relationship desires the more men seem to be checking me out. It's as if they now think I've got some new stuff between my legs as well. Join the exes. Dream on! I'm literally driving down busy Cicero Avenue returning from the office and a big eighteen wheeler truck is slowing, while the driver is making gestures at me. Really. He is out of his mind if he thinks that I am going to endanger myself to cross over lanes to turn off the busy street just to talk with him. He's probably up to no good anyway. Men. My girlfriend Gina says I'm beginning to sound disgruntled these days. Humph, easy for her to say. She's not amongst the jungle.

Maybe Gina is right. I am obviously, truly disappointed in the date scene, but still have hope that I will find love again. Keeping busy with the boys and indulging in pleasantries for me may suffice momentarily, but the mere fact that we all get lonely for adult companionship is enough to understand that it isn't as easy as I make it look. I yearn to be held and touched just like those that are getting theirs on the daily basis, but once you've been settled and comfortable in your relationship or marriage, how soon we forget the lonely syndrome we all know all too well.

My surgery distracted me from any male dealings, but now a sistah's emotions have kicked in full blast. I'm too mature and have way too much respect for myself to indulge in improper behavior with any of my exes just to take care of my building urges. I truly love

SEX! It's just that with it, comes a lot of unexpected feelings and someone ends up hurt if simply done on a whim. Every man I've been intimate with knew it was on once we'd gone there. They probably thought to themselves damn, I'm in this thing deeper than I'd thought. That is correct. "THE RELATIONSHIP GIRL," None of these cookies without it. You might as well sign on the dotted line for the time being and pretend, "I Do!"

So if you think for one minute you can put me on a shelf and come back periodically for a tightening up call, think again.... Some of my friends think I'm crazy, but I don't judge them. It may kill me not to have a relationship at times because of my sexual appetite, but the one thing many have learned is I refuse to settle. I see so many women stay in relationships that they can't stand just to retort, "I got a man." Really. Why should I allow someone to waste my time? If we are not on the same page, Adios. As I've gotten older I notice my tolerance for bull has lessened. Cute doesn't mean a hill of beans if your cute ass is going to cause havoc for me. I will take a mediocre man with great personality that loves him some Nicole any day. It's funny because I can see why many people are single. I have diagnosed myself and feel refreshed for my next beau.

Chapter Twelve
It's Raining, Storming yet, Still Looking for Sunshine

I'm out with my friends that I frequently took on the dance spots with, Casey and Tracy. We are dancing our butts off and ooh wee, I spot a chocolate dancing machine that literally stops my focus. He's not cute, simply ordinary, but he has caught my interest with his smooth style on the dance floor. Tracy comes waving in my face blocking my view, "Girl, one of your exes here? You look fixated on something."

"How about, you are blocking my view from that chocolate, tall brother out there working it."

"You are so silly, Niki. Go say something."

"You know I'm a little shy."

"Girl, get over it. That's why you don't have anybody, now."

"Whatever."

"Girl, He's coming this way." He walks straight up to me, excuses himself to my girlfriend and asks for me to accompany him on the dance floor. I'm blushing and feeling nervous all in one. "Sure." We are dancing to the infamous house music from our error. The DJ is hot. He is really blowing the tables up. The ambiance is perfect, great music, charming guy and chemistry flowing. After the dance we introduce ourselves and head off the floor. I notice that he now, is kind of lingering around my friends and I. Another popular house cut comes on and he's pulling me back to the floor.

We're maneuvering through the crowd and back to the dance floor working it out. This time he's smiling at me and me at him. We continue dancing and giving eye contact as if there is no tomorrow. My hair is wet and beads of sweat have formed on his forehead. "What a workout," I say with a smile.

"Yeah, I'm just getting started, girl." We both laugh and speak on how we aren't as young as we use to be. He walks me back to the table where my friends are looking appreciatively. A little more small talk emerges and we decide to exchange numbers. He gives me a quaint hug and his regrets upon leaving as he expresses an early start for work the next day. I express understanding and the nice meeting you spill.

Casey looks at me and says, "Girl, he was cute. I hope you got his number."

"I did." We both look at each other and giggle. Tracy looks me over with her umhmm, mothering look. "So, what's wrong with this one?"

I hunch my shoulders and retort, "I don't know, hopefully nothing."

"If things don't fly you know I'm going to question your picky behind. He was looking at you and totally feeling you." Something tells me that Tracy isn't on my team with this dating ordeal anymore. She seems to think that it is me. We enjoy the rest of the evening dancing, joking and checking out the brothers. I can't help, but think about Tracy's statement. What is wrong with him? I quickly dispel the thought and think, who knows maybe he is actually on something.

One day passes and neither of us has broken down and phoned the other. I give him a call and break the monotony of who makes the first call. I figure, he did ask me to dance. So, technically he made the first move. I find myself on the phone truly enjoying his conversation for at least a couple of hours. He doesn't seem as if he wishes to end our conversation. I tell him I would love to talk again and he says let's do a meal together. I'm instantly excited. Wow, the brother wants to meet up with me after a night of dancing during our initial meet and a couple hours of conversation. I tell him let's make it happen. He runs his few errands and I tie up loose ends with my children and a few hours later we meet at a Mexican Restaurant. He looks at me curiously in effort to figure out what I plan to order. He's surprised when I order Chiles Rellenos. He orders the typical burrito. While waiting we toast with a couple of Margaritas. The conversation is casual and I'm not sure if he is vibing with me as he did the evening we met.

He expresses during conversation that he simply dates. I ask for more explanation regarding the comment and he explained that he is not dating exclusively.

He says, "you know we all have to eat so why not be able to call someone up for a nice meal and conversation without strings attached?"

"Wow." In the back of my mind I'm prejudging at this point. He obviously makes a decent salary. He drives up to the restaurant with a shiny new Lexus wearing designer cut jeans, nice white button up collar shirt that accents his chocolate skin all so well and pricey alligator boots. He wants a friend with benefits setup.

"Damn." After the meal we hug good bye and head our separate ways. Deep down inside I know that the relationship girl is not his style. Disappointment overwhelms. Days, weeks and still haven't heard from the dancing machine. Casey called and I explained to her what happened and she expressed how she's been there not too long ago and how irritating the dating scene is. She says her sister doesn't get it because she has been with her husband since college. I break down and call Tracy to give her the bad news before she talks to her sister and she is utterly in disbelief.

"What did you say to him?"

"Nothing, Tracy, he just wasn't that into me."

"Wow, well I don't know." She said it with this can't believe you are still messing things up with these men out here, matter of fact attitude.

"You can't work things out with that last guy?"

"Um No, I'm not desperate. Things will pan out eventually."

"Girl, I hope so." I find myself not even mentioning the men I meet to family and friends because their disappointment can be just as big as yours. I only gave my sister friends the courtesy of knowing the outcome because they were with me at the time of the encounter. It's best to keep things to myself until something significant arises. As I recollect thoughts of many disappointments I've had to digest, the thought comes across of the many women that experience crude, crazy and dissatisfying results from the date escapade. So many women have become so disgruntle and without hope. I just believe that nothing comes easy and this one better be well worth it when he arrives.

As much as I hate to admit it, this single thing is not my idea of fun. I've experienced a few disappointments and some hurtful heartaches, but something tells me it will all be worth it. My man is coming. I know I haven't been the most open minded sistah, but some of the less desirables that filter my way should know they don't have a chance with a decent, more polished woman as myself. It's like seriously, you honestly think you will get play from me with those raggedy teeth? Or tattoos on your neck?

Maybe pants sagging from your butt are going to intrigue me? Let's not forget the non-articulate brothers. I is, those pants is, the womens out here, as if I could. Speak English for crying out loud. I am by far a snob, but I do have expectations of the male representative that stands before me. I think of things that I can do to better myself so why not expect others that step your way to be at least presentable. I am not a stickler for a certain size male. Preferably he would be at least five foot ten, hair or without (no receding half way past the middle of your hair line), no toothpicks (healthy women like me need something to hold on, too) stomach is ok as long as you don't appear to be a pregnant male, common sense a must, handy other than the bedroom and self-sufficient. Meaning you are doing great on the salary or hourly rate you make. He must be willing to balance his time because there's nothing more important than a man that wants to incorporate you into his life and wishes to engage into yours.

I truly don't believe that I am asking for much. I believe the best thing I have going for me is not giving up hope in finding a special someone just for me. Settling is for the incapable. That will never be me. My Sunshine is definitely heading my way. Some wonder how I keep my drive, but I know that the "Real" is that God didn't make me a punk. I'm a driven woman that will see my destiny through. I am meant to have my King. Of course, I get discouraged at times, but faith keeps me in power mode. My feelings of fear, yet hope.

***

I fear the decisions I must make for the reality is my life alone is not the only one at stake…the glimmer in my sons' eyes as they see me come through the door helps me stay focused and know what must be in store…can't settle for half ass with no intentions for more can't sleep on emotions only wishing to score… the beauty of love is compromise galore… in my heart I still hope for the fantasy and much more, but the agony of anticipation is yet, more than I can bare…affixed stare and wonderment peeking through my eyes, while holding my breath in the air hoping never to be looked upon negatively with contentment and despair…awaiting the appreciation for fine art glaring through the eyes…seeing improvement and the delight of delicacy promoting an upward rise…finding things work out in the long run creating much bliss and much surprise.

Chapter Thirteen

Sunshine

I have come to a conclusion that sometimes it's just not your time to love. I've done everything from online to personal friends and family hookups. My poor mother is distraught because for the life of her she can't understand why there isn't a "Good Man" selecting to be with her child. A month ago she even took the liberty of hooking me up with a manager of her favorite wholesale store. When I say favorite, I mean favorite. My mother should have stock in Cam's Wholesale. She took it upon herself to nose around in some seemingly nice man's business enough to confirm he was single. She showed him pictures of me and from her description all sounds good.

After much persuading, I go to the wholesale store to meet this gentleman. He was attractive, yet not quite what I would have selected for myself. He was a fair complexion just like mine and was of average height. However, as I get older I have become more open minded to the term, thinking outside of the box. We stood in the store talking and feeling one another out for a good thirty minutes before I decided to ask the magic question, "Are you single or available shall I say?"

"Well, I'm definitely single, but I've got a friend that I can call for some things and vice versa."

"Really, sounds like you are a very good catch from all you've expressed, but it also sounds as if you have a woman."

"No, it's not my woman. If she was my woman, she would have access to some of my personal things, like my house."

"Oh wow, that's truly interesting. Well, on that note I'm going to finish getting the items I came here for and it was nice meeting you." I literally wanted to kick myself for meeting this guy because he reminded me of that lying Orlando. The thought came across my mind that I had actually given him my card during a pause in the conversation before asking him the big question and he diligently phoned my cell phone right in front of me as if to give proof that he was going to call me. I have not heard from him since and honestly, I'm glad. I can't do another cheater or player type.

It is one of those days when a sistah just don't feel like prettying herself. I am frumpy as all get out with leggings, flip flops and a raggedy t-shirt on my way to my sister's house to bring her the bag she'd left at our last family celebration and who do I bump into other than the guy that said no to me. I'd done a meet and greet with him a couple of years ago and he seemed to have really liked me, but days later it was expressed that even though he was attracted to me he had been talking to a few others on line and had engaged in meets with them and had narrowed his selection down to getting to know only one woman at a time. He expressed that although he felt a vibe between us he also, liked another woman he'd previously met online as well. He said, he'd felt it would only be fair to give it a shot with her because he'd met her first. He expressed being smitten with both of us, but wasn't up for game playing and truly wasn't trying to put himself or the woman he dealt with in a hurtful situation. That's funny because although I too, was exploring other options besides him it still didn't feel good to know that he had decided on getting to know someone else. I was truly disappointed because I'd felt like we clicked so much over the phone and when I saw him, I wasn't repulsed. He wasn't bad on the eyes at all. Not to mention, he looked at me like he couldn't believe I was interested in him. My reserved, yet demure demeanor set in right away. Something about a love interest that might actually work for me gets me all tied up in knots and nervous. The chemistry felt on that first meeting was definitely good. Couldn't believe I wasn't the chosen one. Why, oh why had I decided to stop for gas before visiting with my sister. Dang. He's probably thinking I surely made the right decision. Look at me I'm a mess. I was wishing at that very moment that I had swapped out the raggedy T-shirt for a more flattering, sexy blouse and threw the darn flip flops to the side for a nice size heeled shoe. Of course, leggings are a big legged girl's best friend. Simply hot. I pushed aside my negative thoughts and held my head up high, straightened my posture and strutted right up to him with the most dazzling smile I could display. Although I wasn't looking my best, my attitude was giving nothing away. My confidence was portrayed in my stance and reflected in my optimal glance.

"Well, hello Nicole."

"Hi, Seal."

"You look good, girl. What's been going on with you?"

"Thank you, nothing much, just a little of this, a little of that."

"So, are you seeing anyone?"

"Ah, just doing a little dating here and there. How are things going with you and the lady you decided to pursue?"

"Wow, after a couple of weeks of talking to her I found out she was getting to know my boy that I work with. He thought she was really into him as well. I normally don't mention my personal business, but when he inquired, I decided to share and all hell broke loose. It's funny because he was the main reason I'd got on an online site in the first place. He'd expressed coming across some decent women and at the time I'd been divorced for a couple of years with no luck out here on the street."

"I'm so sorry to hear that."

"I would've called you because I truly liked you, but felt you would feel slighted because I'd decided to get to know only one person and I'd met her first."

"No, although I was disappointed, I was also, feeling out other suitors so, I understood."

"Well, is there a chance for me to call you and start over? I mean we did see something in each other then, maybe we can see what else we have in common other than attraction. I do understand that you are dating, but correct me if I'm wrong, you don't sound as if you are exclusive with anyone at this time."

I giggle, "I am not. I talk to a few guys on the phone and have gone out here and there, but nothing promising or confirmed to be a go with any of them."

"So, does that mean you will give me another chance to pursue you?"

"Hmmm, I suppose we can see where things land. There won't be any second runner ups again, will there? Considering you chose the second runner up over the first in your last chance." We both break into laughter. My phone began to ring and it's my sister wondering where I am. I'd totally forgotten that she'd been waiting on me. I hang up and turn to Seal and give him a farewell hug. He smiles and assures me he will be phoning me tonight so that we can continue our conversation. As I enter my sister's home she is looking at me strange. "What is that silly grin on your face about?" I flush at the thought of what just transpired and let out a big sigh. I immediately avoid the subject at hand and began questioning my sister about something new in her home. Past experiences tell me to keep my mouth shut and see what happens. You see, things just haven't been favorable for me in the last couple of years and rather than have everyone go through another disappointment I will see where this thing goes first. Actions are needed to confirm the so called interest expressed. Seal has to follow through with a call.

Brenton and Kendall engaged in video games and I am cooking dinner when my cell phone rings with an unfamiliar number. I immediately think, those darn solicitors are always bugging people. I answer with a little irritation in my voice and detect a familiar, yet, friendly voice. It's Seal.

"Did I catch you at a bad time?"

"No, I didn't recognize the number so I figured it was a salesperson or wrong number."

"Really," he pauses for a minute and sounds disappointed as he states, "you deleted me from your contacts?"

"Um, Yes."

"Wow, I figured I'd get kudos for being a nice guy and being truthful with you."

"Look, we are starting anew and I didn't save your number because I figured you were set with your new person and there was really no need for us to keep in touch."

"Yeah, I suppose I understand that."

"Good, let's talk about you. What are things that I should know about you? What do you enjoy?"

"Oh ok, that's easy." Seal began to tell me all about his aspirations He expresses going back to school in order to keep up with the latest revisions and upgrades in his field. He's a project manager for a major company. All I recall is the field of study entails computer knowledge. Everything else he shared regarding his career is a blur. He tells me of his children and his active relationship with them.

I'm delighted by this information because it confirms that he isn't a dead beat father like Brandon. I listen on to his numerous stories of his life and what has given him drive. I find myself intrigued by his eloquent speech. He truly speaks so articulately. I'm impressed. The conversation shifts gears and he began to tell me what he wishes to have in a woman. He talks about women with old fashion values that do not mind cooking a meal and keeping things tidy. He has me laughing as he tells stories of women that he has dated that knew nothing about the kitchen let alone cooking a classy or traditional dish for her man. The homes of some of these women are enough to repulse any man that believes in simple hygiene practices and clean surroundings. He explains that so many women just do a quick clean and hit the streets never looking back to holding things down around the homestead. He speaks of not wanting his woman in the party scene twenty-four/seven. Seal states that he understands that everyone needs an outlet, but every night, every weekend, whenever someone calls can be over the top. "I just want someone that will be able to have balance in their life. Friends and hanging out is fine with moderation, but the needs of the family and intimate relationships in my opinion should be put first. I'd like a woman that is open minded and willing to try different things, such as; foods, places, and new ideas. I want for her to always be mindful that how you retrieve something is how you keep it. I want her to work with me to keep our relationship spicy and forth going. I hope that she will be able to accept being a lady and allow me to treat her as such. So many women today do not know how to act like a lady. They seem to feel that they have to be hardened. I like my woman refined and lady like." My mouth is gaped open as I listen to this man describe the woman I believe I am. He pauses after a mouthful and asked if I had any inquiries and if he sounded a little over the top with his wish list.

I gasped and simply replied, "not at all."

"Well, Nicole what's your deal and what exactly do you hope to find in a mate?" I think about the question for a minute before responding because he has just described me and what he expresses as his desires are exactly what I'd want from the man that I'd wish to be with. "Hmmm, let's see, I am currently engaging in all types of fun activities to keep myself entertained and also, holding down the fort as a full-time single parent for my boys. I am not privy to breaks every other weekend because my ex-spouse does not come around much. As far as a companion, I'd like a mate that is compassionate, compromising, and real. I would like for him to be mellow in a sense, but not too reserved that he isn't able to enjoy himself in a variety of settings. I'd hope that he can see beyond the external presence of me and would be able to connect intuitively with me. I say this because so often we connect on the physical appearance of a person alone and never see beyond that.

Hopefully, he would gain the respect of my sons and be able to contribute a man's insight on life in a positively reflective way. Of course, if the man is treating me special, the lesson I hope for them to gain is foreseen. I believe that no matter who I decide to be with I must have respect for him because without it the relationship is doomed. I want him to bring out my sexy and womanly qualities in every way possible. Self-sufficient is a deal breaker. If he can't take care of himself we have nothing to talk about. Most of the qualities that you've expressed, Seal are simply qualities that I possess and the man that looks for those qualities is the man that would entertain the thoughts of being with someone like me. I felt like your wish list of a woman very closely resembles that of mine for a man."

"Wow, Nicole you have it understood. You actually seem to get it." Seal pauses for a moment and says, "I know I'm not the best looking man, I mean I'm not a model, but I think I can still turn a head or few. Are you attracted to me physically?"

"Seal, I think that I'm attracted to the total you. You seem to have integrity and your openness to communicate delights me on a whole new level." I think to myself, he is an average looking male, but the attraction I have for him is the quality of the man that I believe him to be, not to mention he has the sexiest expressions that come across his face. I wouldn't describe him as fine or cute. That does not fit him or his image at all. He is attractive, but not in the way of the norm. I'd have to say overall he is just the icon for Sexy. If only he knew how sexy his conversation was. Intelligence is such a turn on for me. The more we get to know each other, the more I feel my attraction for him heighten. Something is so sexy about him. The lure of his eyes as they look at me causes my private sanctuary to tingle when he is near me. I don't know what's destined to be, but I am truly digging me some Seal. As we continue to converse, Seal changes his pace to prompting ideas for a very first date. Or shall I say a very first, second time around date. I will not forget that we've started down this road before and he went with the alternate plan of seeking out someone else. He decides he wants to take me to a seafood restaurant that of course everyone speaks highly of. In my mind, I'm playing things cool because while I'm digging him and all, a sistah has not forgotten the last time we did this thing ending with decisions to cease contact with me.

I quickly, dismiss my negativity and before agreeing, ask if he's sure he doesn't want to just meet for coffee to feel one another out more first. He ignores my cynical comment and says rather joyfully, "So what's it going to be Seafood dinner with me or continued torture of one of the biggest mistakes of my life?"

I smile into the phone and respond, "I forgive you, Seafood it is."

"Nicole, I never expressed it, but I regretted the decision of selecting to seek her out first, moments after I'd told you. The thought of us not conversing anymore was not easy. I think that the mere fact that we liked each other as individuals should have been our focal point. I'm so sorry."

Wow. I wasn't really trying to make him feel bad. I feel all warm and sensitive inside. "Seal, it's fine. It said a lot about your character. Truthfully, it helped me to believe in good men again. You willingness to be honest and not play games with multiple women's hearts intrigued me. It made you appear above the rest."

"Excellent, so glad you appreciate me for the man that I am. So, what day works for you?"

I think about the days I have engagements with friends or with my boys and respond anxiously, "Friday." We converse a little longer and deep down inside I feel as if I know that we have made a connection with one another. The anticipation of meeting up with him for dinner this week has me nervous. I find myself doing mental self-talk after the conversation has ended. "Nicole, you can do this. Stop being afraid. Every man is different and you won't know if he is true unless you give him a chance. Find your balance." Whew! It's a wrap. Everything will be fine.

The restaurant is absolutely charming. The ambiance is to die for. Wow, this man actually has taste. Imagine that. So this is the hoopla everyone is buzzing about. As we approach our table, Seal quickly pulls my chair out for me. The menu appears to be quite expensive. I wonder if he takes all of the women he date out to expensive restaurants. He looks at me with curious eyes as I search for something to appease me. Can't go wrong with Tilapia. I decide on Fried Tilapia and shrimp meal and listen intently as he rattles off appetizers that include something foreign to my taste buds. Alligator bites... He then, selects his choice of cuisine. "I will have the Red Fish with wild rice and asparagus along with a separate container of Cajun Wine Sauce." I was impressed. A man that has exquisite taste. I felt a little too safe with my Fried Tilapia dish. When the appetizers arrive he is delighted to see that I indulged in the Alligator Bites and to his surprise, I enjoyed the different taste. A delicacy indeed.

We sit and gaze as one another shares stories of childhood experiences and barely eat the food ordered. After our food is packaged he walks me to the car and before opening my door pins me to the door planting a wet kiss on my mouth. I look at him surprised and he then, hesitates and again, presses his mouth onto mine slightly opening his in order to passionately devour my tongue. Seal tugs at my body pulling me into him and caresses my back gently while holding me tightly. I was not only shocked, but enticed by the excitement riveting through my body. He releases me reluctantly and I stumble into my car. I could barely contain myself as I drove home. Something about him felt real. I make it home safely and quickly text him thank you for the great evening out and assure him that I'd made it home safely. He returns the text and states that he waits for the moment we see each other again. I have teenage-likebutterflies. The next evening after we've both settled in from work we once again engage in a lengthy conversation. We discuss our families, careers, social lives and other affiliations we are connected too. He speaks of his children with true concern and love for them. It makes me think of the loser of a husband I'd married that barely connects with his children. Seal speaks of his diligence in retrieving his son and daughter biweekly. He expresses that no matter what the occasion their scheduled time with him is not broken. I respect a man that takes care of his responsibilities. He expresses that family is very important to him. I tell him about my relationship with my sons and express that my son's wish for their mom to be content and happy.

"Awe, would that have anything to do with the fact that your ex-husband has remarried?" I think to myself, how smart is he?

"Absolutely" I answer. We go back and forth for a while telling of our children and then, move on to the careers we've gotten ourselves in. The vibe between us is truly unreal. A month passes by so quickly and before we know it we discuss meeting one another's children. The thought scares me after the last man that the children allowed themselves to get close, too. That darn Greg has truly scarred me. I have to trust again. I look the man that I've been heavily dating over the last month square in the eye and tell him, let's do this. Seal has his children every other week so of course that means the introduction of Brenton and Kendall is first. I know that my sons will like him simply because I like him. I feel afraid. I think back to Brenton texting Greg and expressing that he was the best man his mom has ever had. My poor son was begging and pleading for this inconsiderate ass to resume a relationship with his mom. The thought has me fuming. Poor little Kendall hardened and resulted to senseless name calling of the formerly liked, Greg. Oh my God, what am I bringing this poor man into? Will Seal be able to pull it off? Seal appears at my home ready to meet the boys and Brenton quickly asks him if he'd like to see his lizard. Seal responds, "Sure, go get him." Brenton happily returns with his pet lizard in his hand. Seal picks him up and just like that Brenton accepts him as being pretty cool.

"Wow!" Kendall speaks, but doesn't say much. I think back to how chatty he was with Greg. I become worried. Seal assures me everything will be just fine. "Give it time." I know he's right, but can't help but worry. I love his confidence though. I worry about what his children may think of me, but more importantly his mother. I tell you the man is adamant about the getting to know the kid thing first. The weekend after meeting the boys approaches quickly. It just so happens that the week in which I introduce Seal to my sons leads to a child free weekend for him. He takes it upon himself to plan a kid date for my sons and me. This has got to be the most thoughtful thing a man has ever done to truly connect with my boys. That is without a hidden agenda.... The boys are quiet on the way to the museum that Seal decides to take us to. They admit that they are excited to see all the cool science exhibits, but resist in saying too much on the ride there. Seal is engaging with the boys and just as silly as we are as a whole. The boys are enjoying the outing with Seal. By the time we get to the restaurant, Seal has planned the boys are chatting with him as if they've known him all along. I'm loving every minute of this and feeling even more connected with Seal. Oh wow, things with the boys went great. It's Sunday. I totally forgot that I agreed to meet Seal's mother today. Oh shoot, every dress in my closet all of a sudden seems to be short. What will she think of me? Hot Mama! Dang, think Nicole, what is stylish enough for the new boyfriend yet, classy enough for mom? I've got it my favorite dress. It's not matronly, but cleavage is contained and it's still a little short to keep Seal looking. Not to mention, I am and always will be a leg girl. Every woman must always keep in mind their asset. I even have a more conservative shoe to wear. Ha. I'm good. I think to myself, confidence is a must and this dress is truly confident. I arrive at Seal's house and the look on his face confirms I've done well. As we pull up to the church, Seal looks at me with concern.

"Are you ready to meet my mom, Sweetie?"

"That, I am." He looks at me and smiles and I affectionately look at him returning the smile. He must know that I am nervous as can be. Of course, I prance into the church poised and confident as if to have not a worry in the world. The church is quaint, but cozy. The members appear to be mostly from the surrounding area with some who've following the church over time from location to location. Seal becomes excited as he spots his sister and her family. I nudge him saying, "I thought it was just mama." He smiles and says, "Sweetie this is such a treat. You now get to meet my sister that taught me most of what I know about women and my expectations of them." Are you serious? I have to meet the sister he speaks so highly of. Oh wow. I all of a sudden feel nervous more so than before. I meet his niece who flaunts a pink and green scarf during the church's Fellowship Embrace. I knew instantly that she was the niece that he informed me was my sorority sister. How beautiful and sweet this young lady was. I had to pry just a little to get the family dynamics sought out and just as I figured a smarty as well. Hmm, good genes must run in the family. As I turn to go back to the pew where we sat, Seal summons for me to return to meet his uncle and nephew. The uncle was reserved and offered a hand shake, whereas the nephew was very outspoken, but a delight to hear. He spoke so openly about his uncle being a great guy and even threw a couple of threats my way in which we all resulted to giggles. I liked him a lot. His niece actually reminded me of myself when I was her age. To think back to the age of college places a smile across my face.

While sitting in the pew glancing and smiling at one another, Seal whispers in my ear, "Are you ready to meet mom and big sis?"

I chuckle, "Of course." After church has ended, the sweat on my forehead begins to bead. An older woman and another woman the mere image of her walk our way.

"Well, this must be Nicole."

"We have heard so much about you." I blush with pure delight that Seal has told them about me. I begin to utter, "Likewise" as the sister pulls me into an embrace. Seal's mom is still sizing me up, but I can tell she likes me. I'm so relieved that his family is so expressive and welcoming.

His mom blurts out, "she is pretty and looks like someone I would've chosen for you. Not to mention, Seal tells me you are a smart, together young lady."

Again, I blush.

"You seem to be such nice people. I now see where Seal gets it from."

"Well, thank you. I suppose I have done something right in raising this gentleman. It was truly nice meeting you, hope we see you at some of our upcoming family gatherings."

"It was nice meeting you all and I hope to see you again soon."

As we parted there was a series of hugs given and a feeling of relief that I had made it through the meeting of some of Seal's family. Whew. In the car, Seal is grinning like a kid in a candy store. "Baby, you are amazing. I truly have a good feeling about us."

I look at him sheepishly and respond, "I take it things look as if they went well at church."

"Yes, you are wonderful. They loved you!" I couldn't help, but smile at him. I now, think of the next hurdle, meeting his children.

The week goes kind of slow. We continue to talk throughout the day and meet up a few times for a brisk walk and breakfast. I'm finding myself more and more excited about my new guy find. He is exactly what I asked for. My worry as of late is the children I'm to meet this weekend. It's my turn to engage and I haven't a clue as to what to do. I ponder on something fun for children to do that will engage all of us. Bowling. That would definitely work. I call to book the bowling alley slot for the weekend only to find that a league is playing all day. Dang. I recall Kendall telling me of a game system that he and his brother play with their dad and his wife. The system is a little pricey, but it will be a good investment for family entertainment plus, it has bowling. This will work because it won't be to odd meeting out and the kids not meshing because they are all out of their comfort zone. My children would love entertaining them. I will order some pizzas and a planned date is done. Of course if the children get bored, I will simply leave it up to Seal. He proves to be the man with the plan. Seal calls to announce their arrival and they are as attractive as the pictures he has shown me. Kyla is very bubbly and energetic. She comes right in with a scroll of questions. Go figure she is her father's child. Too funny. Kyle is just the opposite, he says hello and sits immediately. I engage in general questions with them, but can't quite get them out edge wise with the little news reporter sitting before me. She is seemingly very intelligent, like her father. Kyle warms up a bit and asks where my children were. I invite my children into the front room to engage in conversation with us. Both boys were diligent for once on not letting their first impression of junky rooms be representative of who they are. They gladly came into the living room minutes later with mischievous grins spreading across their faces. Must be a boy thing because Kyle looks as if to resemble the goofiness of their expressions. Kyla tossed her hair and looked the boys up and down asking what they do around here for fun. The boys began to rattle off the games they play and the movies they have and before I knew it my plan of family fun went out the window. The children excused themselves and minutes later were bursting with laughter. Seal and I looked at each other and couldn't believe the silly worrying that overwhelmed us. It is the children that saved us on this venture. Later that evening we all engaged in some family fun and the plan followed through with my planned pizza party. I'm loving this.

The weekend was a success. Now, Seal is excited to meet my family. Lucky for me this weekend is the holiday and my family will be hosting a bar-b-q at my mom's house. I can introduce him to my small family in one setting. Yes, Seal is introduced to everyone immediately. He meets my mother and her mate, their friends, my sisters and my nieces.

Seal engages in conversation, but tends to be a little reserved. Hmm, I am wondering what he is thinking of my family. My sister is very entertaining. Reese talks non-stop all the time. He seems to be actually amused by her. My other sister, Layla is very observant yet, kind of quiet, but she managed to blurt out in front of others if Seal was my new boyfriend. I was surprised, but managed to tell her and her fiancé that we were in the mist of getting to know one another better. In the meanwhile, my youngest niece is tormenting my poor fella with how nice our family is and assuring him that there is no need for him to be nervous. It's actually kind of humorous.

My sons were visiting their dad so it was actually a little easier for me to observe this man in full flair. I believe my family likes him, but I know that they are willing to give anyone that I have given time to a chance. All goes smoothly and I am truly happy. Seal and I exit the yard and proceed to the car once again happy that things went well. It's still early so we decide to rent a movie and take it back to my place before parting. We watched the majority of the movie, but the two of us were destined to start necking at some point. It wasn't long before I noticed Seal looking at me with his bedroom eyes, luring me into his desiring glance. I thought for sure this man would have me tonight, but I forgot about my rule of giving a man hell about the STD check prior to consummating a relationship. It's funny because in the heat of the moment, I can honestly see how the appropriate steps to intimacy go down the drain.

He's been so good about it, unlike others in my past who has given me havoc. He begins to kiss me on my lips and gently inserts his tongue as he caresses my thighs. My body is aching for his attention. I rise slightly so that he is cupping my butt with a firm grip, thrusting me closer to his private sector. I'm alarmed at the major piece of work throbbing near my entrance and I feel like I want to be taken instantly. Seal begins to kiss me on my neck and I'm completely losing it. He tilts my head toward him and kisses my forehead as he looks me in the eye and says, "Sweetie, in due time. We must wait for my test results to clear. I want nothing more, but to devour you with my love and the passion that's in store for you ,but I want you comfortable in knowing that your new man is STD free and ready to explore you freely with no restraints."

My mouth drops open. I want him so bad. I love the way that he has done everything right, but his do right attitude has me feeling like a caged animal ready to attack. I don't believe I've ever desired a man like this before. We continue to view the movie on the tube before us and hold each other tight as if never to let one another go.

Our relationship began so different from most by opening up closed doors that offered us both second chances. It's like we fell for one another each day we spoke in length. I felt the closeness encouraged by every moment spent. I recall our first messages sent during the first encounter meant. I would have never foreseen us parting and meeting again making perfect sense. Our movement is fast and we aren't looking back. I felt scared, but Seal has assured me he won't be leaving me. It's weird these strong feelings acquired in a couple of months, but I'd be certain that something is different and sustained through our love and not simply a hunch. I feel alive and full of joy that God has put this man so compatible here for me. I feel relieved yet, baffled as to where I go now. He likes me just as I am and I'm feeling him as well. Seal tells me there is no slowing down or room to peruse, he wants me now and we are breaking all of the rules. No time restraints or nay says heard just pure love you see, bottled and reserved. Oh, am I feeling this man so. Our dating takes on a smooth yet, upward path and the more time found becomes more time spent. We still can't believe we've stumbled upon one another. Seal and I are so much alike in our thoughts and expectations of life. We connect on a major level more so than any of our predecessors. Our conversations become deeper with every word spoken and people amongst us feel our love. What is this thing that we have and where is this going? I must repel all negatives as I've felt once before to open for chance and feelings galore. I recall the tension of before.

***

So you call yourself smitten, how long will this last…will you continue seeking, and then I'm a blast of the past…I've gotten excited many times before and become more and more reluctant to open up this door…how am I to shield myself from further hurt and pain…do I continue seeking love with such feelings of disdain…you say you wish to know me, I will simply wait to see, if your intentions are that of an honorable man with only pleasures of that of me…I ponder and retract the feeling of joy you bring…suppressing every hear felt song that comes to mind, I only wish to sing…I wish that I could keep you at bay for feeling that our closeness will have you stray …from the unfamiliarity of a woman here truly meant to stay.

***

Three months in and we are more comfortable than ever with one another. I see him for the first time for who he is. He is a good man with extinct character. The excitement is still prevalent, but I've now experienced a serious side to Seal. He expresses that he has shown me that he is here for the duration and wishes to continue to be with me. I flash back to my doubts of us lasting due to my own internal fears. I recognize him as true now and all fears have fallen adrift. I'm secure in my place with him and he seems to believe in my feelings for him. We've decided that getting to know one another inside out and developing a comfort level were our first steps to a binding relationship. We've managed to keep our sanity and indulge in each other in every possible way, drawing us closer and closer without consummating our relationship. The overwhelming desire is becoming more irresistible than ever. We long for each other and yet, still find ways to satisfy the need to embrace and simply be close. I know that he desires me, but love that he has respected me. His STD check passed with flying colors a month ago, but the on-going flow of the accrued feelings in our every waking moment has been so special that we simply wanted things to happen naturally and we both know with having children that our timing means everything. My ex-husband is getting the boys for his tri-annual visit. I mean literally it takes him four whole months before wanting to engage with his boys. Who does that? Seal wishes for me to accompany him to one of his friend's engagement party. I'm wondering what I have in my closet that will fit this occasion. I follow my closet through each descript section; sexy and after five, girly and playful, matronly and church appropriate, business casual and professional. Hmmm, I'm guessing a twist of sexy and definitely girly. I pull out the perfect dress. It just happens to be one of a few with tags still hanging. Seal will love this dress. It reveals a little cleavage, but not drastic and it wraps around my body with a tie on one side. It flounces playfully around my hip as I walk. The perfect shoe is one with straps. I will taunt him for sure tonight.

Brandon is running late picking up our sons, but he at least had the decency to call and assure me he was in route. I've showered and applied my most sensuous fragrance. As I began flat ironing my hair the doorbell rings. Brandon has finally arrived. The boys are packed and I meet them at the door for farewell hugs before they exit. Brandon and I don't take a second look at one another before the door is closed. The feelings of dislike are so apparent. We have our times when we can be civilized with one another ,but this every three to four months visitation is killing my patience for him stepping up to the plate in regards to our boys. Minutes later, I've forgotten the notion of anger that crossed my mind after seeing trifling, Brandon. I'm back in my bathroom doing my hair at a much faster pace because it will be minutes before Seal's arrival. I quickly finish up my hair and throw on my quite girly dress with my strappy shoe and head for a little make up as the doorbell once again rings. I slowly walk to the door only to find the most sexy, chocolate brother standing to greet me. "Seal, baby, you are on time."

"Yes, and happy to see you dressed. You look exquisite."

"Thank you, honey." I'm concealing my excitement, but can't regain focus because Seal is looking so hot. I quickly run to the fridge to get him a beer and then, return to my bathroom to put on the little bit of makeup I laid out on my sink. When I return, Seal is looking at me as if he sees a princess. He places his beer down and takes my hand. When he opens my door there sits a floral arrangement of various hues of red and pink. "Seal, they are gorgeous."

"And so are you, Nicole." I blush at him and off we go to his friend's engagement party. We arrive at this secluded home far out in who knows where and I notice that there isn't any cars parked nearby.

"Seal"

"Yes, honey."

"Um, where are we?"

"Come baby you will be fine." I follow reluctantly. When I get inside there is a huge fire place with flames lit, a cozy sofa sitting before it, a quaint little kitchen and spiraling stairs leading to a master bedroom suite. Wooden beams affixed to the ceilings throughout the home and an all-white bedroom décor with chiffon draping over the bed. Red and pink rose petals are sprinkled throughout. How beautiful. Ella Fitzgerald is playing in the background and a bottle of my very favorite Ice Wine awaits me in a stand filled with ice and to chilled glasses. I can't believe my eyes. Seal is so wonderful. I love this man.

Seal breaks my disbelief as he pulls me closer to him and whispers in my ear, "It's that time baby that I hope to entwine more closely with you, feeling your forbidden sanctuary clasping with mine."

Oh my God, my heart rate has dropped. I'm feeling overwhelmed, excited and floored all in one. The tingly feeling I feel when we kiss is intensified ten times more. Seal leads me to the sofa and pours me a glass of the exquisite wine into my chilled glass. I look at him with much respect and admiration than ever any man before. I allow the sweet music to simmer through my soul and feel him gently moving toward me with the most sensuous look motioning silently for me to meet him with our mere images face to face. We kiss slowly and intimately and quickly pick up our pace. He jumps to his feet and pulls me readily and I follow him with no defeat. We enter the bedroom so beautifully decorated and Seal kisses me slowly as he undresses me. I think to myself, thank goodness I am always trying to be on point because a sistah is most readily dressed to appeal in sexy undergarment attire as well. He's impressed and likes what he sees, his groin area feels full and ready to plunge into me. I feel nervous, but soon forget as he so eloquently handles me. He touches me all over, kissing me, loving me so lavishly. I'm in a world of no recognition, a fantasy now, fulfilled. My Seal has taken me there and back with no regrets or appeals. We engage multiple times until we exhaust ourselves. The embrace is wonderful and so sublime. We comfort each other the rest of the night by holding on to our blissful occurrence we've just shared. I find Seal asleep so peaceful. He looks adorable. I just want to hold him and love him forever. I attempt to creep out of the bed only to find Seal pulling my back down near him. I look at him passionately and climb on top of him. I began kissing and touching him in all the right places and before I know it I've release my wild cat upon him once more. He smiles upon completion and I smirk with disbelief. Our inner glow becomes exposed and I know at this moment there is no turning back. I head to the kitchen to find bagels and bagged coffee ready to prepare. We indulge in bagels and coffee before heading back home. The contentment on our faces is clear. We are now, consummated and forthcoming as one.

We continue to thrive in our relationship. Everything just fits. Seal and I find ourselves falling deeper and deeper for each other as our relationship persists. Our lives become so in unison with the children and our family events. We adore each other so much and fitting in time for intimacy has become a constant must. Each intimate encounter is even better than before. We can't keep our distance from one another too long before we want more. Our children are happy and our lives are cohesive. The funny thing is neither of us allows that fire to die. We love each other as if to have been together a lifetime. It's weird how refreshed we both feel to be in a relationship that meets our every status quo. I recall the thoughts I felt when first getting to know Seal…

***

Something Different

I glimpsed at your profile and thought for sure you were something different for me, not my usual, not the ordinary type for sure, you see…but the lure of your personality left me craving for more. More for whatever you had that opened up my door. I feel like you are my soul mate, the soul mate I've never known. Your humor, your articulate speech, confident aura is ongoing and feelings expressed are over flown. You display a for sure confidence that is attracting all alone. Your very own demeanor is like that of my very own clone. I feel nothing, but chemistry when I talk with you on the phone. You challenge me with ongoing debates of believing in my truth, my pessimism and fear of letting go, and my every inquiry to the fullest degree, showing me subtle satisfaction if need be. Proving and showing you're truly delighted by me. There's something rather mystical about you that draws my interest nearer, I think it's the mere image of the male me seen even more clear. Something about you reminds me of the father that I resemble, those personality traits so apparent in thee makes my heart simply tremble. The Aquarian was both my father and me and now comes you, the Aries with our similarities. I adore the mirror of me and you my dear sit center stage. What more can a woman want other than a male who represents her in more ways than he knows, a rare stature that stands before me with my heart sealed and enclosed.

***

Seal suggests dinner at my favorite Thai Restaurant. It's been a whopping seven months on this very day. I wonder if Seal remembers. We arrive promptly at the time of our reservation. We are seated in a dim lit area where mostly couples appear to be. The waiter smiles politely at me as she hands us our menus and dismisses herself. I look at Seal and ask him if there is anything special about today and he raises a brow as if to say wouldn't you like to know.

The candle shimmers light upon our faces as we stare affectionately at each other. Seal finally breaks the silence, "Baby, I know it's only been seven months, but the pleasure of being your man and the feelings of happiness I've experienced since being with you have put the icing on the cake. You truly make me happy and tonight, I just want to celebrate us."

"Oh Baby, you are so good to me and I believe that we are so good for each other. This all makes sense."

I drift into deep thought as Seal summons the waiter over asking him to bring his best bottle of champagne.

My brow arches and I clear my throat, "Honey, did you just say champagne?"

Seal laughs and says, "Yes, Honey it's a special occasion."

The waiter quickly returns and apologetically says, "This is the only Ice Wine we carry. It's our very own brand."

"That is just fine. Thanks for playing along, man."

The waiter smiles and walks away. "Awe, Baby you were just pulling my leg. You truly are the most thoughtful man I have ever been with. I love you." I sit grinning from ear to ear and I see that Seal is so amused. I think of all of the qualities that this man possess and have come to the conclusion that he has every positive of all that preceded him and more. Seal has shown me his spiritual side as we have prayed together numerous times at church and even before our meals. He has compromised his life with his children to blend them with that of mine. He assures me that what's his is mine and what's mine shall be his. Seal places me on a pedestal as if I'm a prized gift found and showers me with affection that confirms my special place with him. My sexy blossoms with him and displays a feeling all of my own. I love to entice his nature until it rises to its fullest height. He brings my sexy more profound than even I could imagine. His honesty resembles that of a good man's character in every story told. Seal shows me a compassion and love that holds strong. My trust in him is believable and warranted. I don't fear my indulgence in him because I truly believe he will last.

Seal and I enjoy our delicious food and continue to talk over dinner. We are both so stuffed. Seal ask the waiter if he could prepare our leftovers for take home containers. Seal and I return to my home with our remains. Before we enter the house, Seal's face turns to concern and my heart skips a beat. "Is everything ok, Sweetie?"

"Nicole, please take a seat on the porch with me." I'm thinking what has gotten into this man. He is concerned and aloof after such a nice meal. I'm sure our combined clan has torn the house upside down. I sit down and concern has now over taken my face. He smiles delicately and says that he is not ready to share our moment of just being together this evening just yet. We sit in silence on the bench on the front porch staring in the sky. Seal ruffles through our bags and pulls out a fortune for him and one for me. His has blue markings on it and mine pink. We open our fortunes to share as we've done many times before and the most beautiful ring exposes itself at first crack of the seal. Seal looks at me with the most caring, loving and desiring eyes and kneels down on one knee and says, "Nicole, you are the love of my life. Please have me as yours." I have completely melted into pieces. Seal takes the ring from me and places it on my finger as I burst into tears, slurring "Yes, baby Yes, I will have you." Our embrace is long and the joys of our hearts have met.

We enter the house and an explosion of congrats have hit the door. Seal has over done himself. Our family and close friends have entertained and partied on our behalf in recognizing our future marital bliss. Seal is amazing. We look at one another and shake our heads as we mix and mingle through hugs, kisses and still more embraces. Our families are happy and so are we. Our love story has only just begun.

***

The WILL to Love

The will to Love makes my heart skip a beat at the very moment I anticipate our very meet… the Will to love has me mesmerized by the mere thought of his every expression that smoothly seems to emerge in my mind… every time I hear him speak, my mind and body becomes weak…the moment I'm near him my heart flutters and my inner passion for him grows…the funny thing is I don't think he knows…When I lie down to sleep, he dominates my thoughts and tremors run down my body as I imagine him near me, kissing, hugging and touching me so dearly…the Will to Love has me caught by surprise, forgetting of any past nonsense or all of which I despise… the Will to Love has me assured of a happy future with him in my life; no drama, or ignorance, not even strife…I adore him, respect him and believe in his word, hoping clearly that all will stay good with no matters of discern…the Will to Love has brought satisfaction of a gem found with no remorse and only upward thrust…the mutual understandings and desires of we make all things vibrant and so very clear to see…the Will to Love is my most wished for companion and heart's desire, I thank God for he that brings such joy and delight to me…the Will to Love has released my doubt and untwined the sunshine throughout.

Epilogue

Life with Sunshine

Seal and I are getting ready for our big day. A relative of his family has blessed us with being our officiator of marriage. I can't believe the day is already here. It's a beautiful day and all of our guests are waiting. Seal and I decided to do a rather quaint yet, small ceremony. The church is decorated in hues of Red and Pink. Our children are an important part of our lives and it is their honor to stand beside the two of us and give our hand in marriage to one another. Seal is standing before me, what a handsome display. I look forward to being with him for the rest of his days. He glances at me, giving me a wink. My heart dances with Amore'. I know our love will prove the test of times. I look forward to our days together. Seal promises me everything with us will always be ok.

ABOUT THE AUTHOR

Angela Cross is a professional educator and counselor residing in Chicago, Illinois. She obtained a bachelor's degree in elementary education and later a master's degree in the psychological area of guidance and counseling. Angela is a member of the very prominent sorority, Alpha Kappa Alpha Sorority, Inc. Angela was married for 11 years from which she acquired the birth of two sons, Dylan and Nyles, the joys of her life. She has always found love in writing expressions of feelings. Most of her inspiration is developed through a number of personal experiences as well as experiences sought out through the lives of others. She hopes that her stories will entertain and enlighten readers in her audience. Visit Angela at www.angelacross.net